ASPECTED

The Emperor's Conscience, Book 1

MICHAEL K. COMBS

Longship Publishing, LLC

Acknowledgements

I would like to thank some people who really helped make the most out of this book. I am grateful for you!

Anna - The talent and artistry behind my covers. Her skill and keen eye gave my book a life of it's own.

Cameron - My editor, who helped me actualize the vision I had in my head and called me on my B.S. whenever he caught me cheating.

Thank you both. You are the best!

I dedicate this book to Jon Rumsey, who convinced me that my stories were good, and needed to be told.

Be careful what you ask for, my friend.

JOIN MY VIP LIST

VIP Membership puts you on the front lines to receive the latest news, updates on upcoming novels, free books and giveaways, and behind the scenes information regarding new releases and more.

See the back of the book for information on how to sign up.

Prologue

Blessed Queen. In the end, we find beginning. In the beginning, we find home. Born of you and received by you, what turmoil in this life I have known so to make me who I am. Not fate, but choice decided this path of pain until I am left wondering if what little good I have done was worth my soul. Seeking peace in a life well lived and finding only destruction, may I look toward my death as the end of my journey, to rest.

Prayer excerpt from a sermon delivered by Del Iningar, Celate of the Temple of Hessa, Corin, Pre-Empire—Moments before he took his own life.

In the Beginning

My first memory, aside from the nightmares, is of being bathed. I was six years old when the man with the kind face carried me to the Temple of Hessa. The large copper tub swallowed me, and I could barely peek above the rim as he scrubbed my skin with a cloth. The air was thick with the scent of lye, and every so often, he would pause in his work and rinse the rag in the pink water.

"There now, Evanar," he said as he scrubbed an arm. "I'm sure that feels much better." Occasionally he'd mumble something like, 'Don't be afraid,' or, 'There are other boys and girls here, and I am sure you will be great friends.' These statements were meant to ease my mind, though at the time I didn't know why he felt the need.

When he made such comments, I would scrunch up my brow. Why would I be afraid? And who was Evanar? Was he referring to me? He must have been, for I knew no name for myself.

"Evanar?" I said hesitantly. They were the first words that I had spoken since I arrived.

"Yes, my boy. Your name is Evanar. Mine is Tamil. Tamil Haran," he said with a smile, then he started, eyes wide in realization. "Though you ought to have a last name, too, I think." This part he mumbled to himself. "Never thought to ask, damn my hide."

He began muttering names then, slowly at first, as if tasting them. Finding them unpleasant, he would grimace and toss them aside. He finished one arm and began on the other. He would mention a name, tell a story associated with that name, or shake his head and tell me about how he had once known someone by that name, but they were an ass so he wouldn't saddle me with something like that. Then he'd chuckle and reminisce about old friends.

He told me stories as he leaned his forearms on the side of the tub and I soaked. He told them, one after another, until the water began to cool. He finally shook himself and started washing the dried red mud from my legs, and said, "Hostric Agon. Now that was a fine fellow. A talented fighter, a wise man…" he sighed heavily, "And a good friend. Yes. It's settled. You will be Evanar Hostric."

When he scrubbed the bottom of one foot with the rag, I giggled and kicked out, splashing the pink water furiously and soaking his face and robes. He let out a bellow of a laugh as the water dripped from his neatly trimmed beard, gave me a mock reproving look, then dove after my feet again. The struggle left more water on the floor than in the tub. We were both soaked and out of breath by the time the laughing subsided. Eventually, he had me stand as he poured clean, tepid, water over my head to rinse the remaining blood from my hair and body. He gave me robes of my own to wear. They were itchy. The nightmares came that night.

I RAN.

There were trees all about me as I stalked my prey.

The tiny creature flattened its floppy ears, and I could all but hear its instincts scream at it to flee. But it was not being called to flee me. There were predators about, and they believed, wrongly, that they were the hunters in these woods.

Running full out across the forest floor, I scooped up the small rabbit on the end of one silver talon and tore it in two. Blood sprayed from the small furry body, across the leaf-strewn ground and my own black skin. I tossed the carcass into a small clearing and clawed my way up the nearest tree.

And now I hunt.

I didn't have to wait long. Snuffling sounds came from the thick brush after a few moments. The screech of the rabbit and the scent of fresh blood had drawn them. They could not ignore that scent. Hunger and instinct drew them closer, further into my small clearing —and into my trap.

Four beasts edged into view. The full moon was ample light for my sensitive eyes. The first to enter was the largest. He was larger than me. The giant wolf was clearly the leader. The others flanked him but gave him deference and space. He was cautious, not cowardly. He held his head low to scent the blood and his eyes roamed the surrounding wood for threats.

He found the carcass—my proffered bait. He sniffed it, saliva dripping from his mouth. He cocked his head and sniffed again. His hackles rose at my scent. From the way he turned his wary head, in obvious confusion, I knew that he had never encountered one such as me before. But hunger drubbed his caution, and he took the bait.

As his mouth closed over the rabbit, I dropped from the tree. I landed both silver-taloned feet square on his back. The force was enough to drive him hard to the ground. His breath left in a whoosh, and I dug my talons into his thick fur and clawed him deeply as I leaped from his back and attacked the nearest of his small pack. The giant wolf was a formidable foe, but I was the hunter here and I could take down my quarry. First, though, I had to do away with unnecessary distractions. His pack had to die first.

I hit the nearest wolf, and we tumbled into the small clearing, teeth and claws slashing. The bitch was powerful. Her enormous paw on my chest pinned my shoulders to the ground, and her jaws darted in and out, trying to latch on. I dodged, clawed at her face with a three-taloned hand, and angled my chin under hers. My two rows of razor-sharp teeth found her neck, and I clamped down. I thrashed my head side to side until the flesh parted and she fell limp. I wriggled from under her and spat out the bloody fur and meat and wiped my face with the back of my hand.

Instinctively, I reached out for her shadowy spirit as it left her body. Initially, it streamed from her still form as a vaporous wisp, a living shadow intent on a destination. I seized it. The spirit formed into a likeness of the wolf and turned on me. She snapped her shadowy jaws with no effect. In death, she couldn't touch me, but I could touch her. The feel of the meat in my mouth was unsatisfying, but this—*this*—was what I craved. The energy of the soul. A soul I claimed by right of the hunt. I tried to draw it into myself. I was so hungry. I needed to feed. Hunt and feed. There was nothing else. But when the wolf's spirit came into contact with my own, my whole being convulsed, and I lost the meager contents of my stomach across forest floor. I writhed in pain and released the spirit, burned to my core. The pain subsided immediately.

The painful diversion was enough to give the others a chance to regroup. Another wolf barreled into me, sending me flying from its lifeless pack mate. The others didn't hesitate and pounced before I even hit the ground.

I got a forearm in front of my throat, and powerful jaws latched on. The giant wolf leader had me and pulled hard, keeping me from regaining my feet. Another bit deep into an ankle. I reached out and slashed the muzzle of the leader. He released me with a yelp and with the wolves so much larger than I, I merely had to bend my knee to drag myself closer to the other to kick a taloned foot into the eyes of the last one that held me. I blinded him momentarily. He shook his massive head to clear his vision, but by the time he managed it, I was not where he expected me. I attacked from the flank, wrapping my arms as far around his neck as I could, then dug in my claws and pulled. Skin and muscle tore, blood sprayed in an arc, and in a moment, it too lay still. I watched the spirit leave its body and wisely made no move to take it.

I spun and lashed out with a foot and scored deep gashes in the third's side as he tried to dash around me. He yipped in pain and flinched away. He circled, ears pinned to his head and wary. He looked for weakness. Thinking better of his prospects, he whined toward his leader and limped from the clearing.

Just me and the alpha.

We circled one another. I looked up into his eyes and held his gaze. He did not appreciate it. We lunged at each other and clawed and bit and scratched and punched. He got his jaws around my middle and threw me to the ground. It cost him though, and I left the giant wolf with deep gashes along his neck and face. He circled again. When he lunged this time, I ducked low and dove between his legs. As I hit the ground, I spun to my back, and the massive beast, less nimble than I, could do nothing. I clawed his delicate underbelly with hand and foot. He crashed headlong to the ground and never rose again. I watched his spirit leave his body and my stomach grumbled. I reached out and grabbed the shade. It turned on me, and I thought it would attack me as his mate had. Instead, it looked at me and gave me a nod of acknowledgement for a fight well fought. Then it looked longingly into the forest. It needed to go. I could feel it's insistent tugging. I could not consume this spirit. Even if I could, I wouldn't. I would find other food. Perhaps I would even settle for the meat about the clearing. I released the spirit of the noble beast and gave a primal scream into the night. I was the hunter! I was the predator in these woods.

The last wolf, the one who ran, must have been lurking and seeking an opportunity to attack. When I released my roar of triumph, I heard him run in truth.

Prey runs. I chase.

He ran for all he was worth, but it did him little good. I dragged him down in a small copse of trees and ended him. I felt his spirit pass by me as I collapsed from exhaustion and lost consciousness.

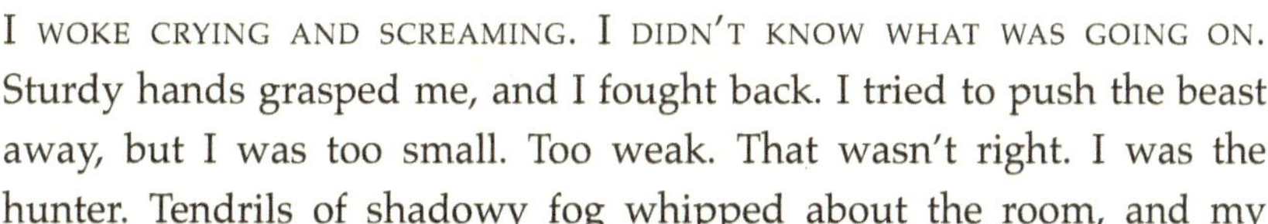

I WOKE CRYING AND SCREAMING. I DIDN'T KNOW WHAT WAS GOING ON. Sturdy hands grasped me, and I fought back. I tried to push the beast away, but I was too small. Too weak. That wasn't right. I was the hunter. Tendrils of shadowy fog whipped about the room, and my vision danced in and out of focus. The beast was growling at me. No. It was speaking.

"Shh. It's okay," it said. "I'm here. You are safe, Evanar. Calm yourself."

I tried to push him away. I pried at his hands and beat him with my fists, but it was no use. He pulled me close. He had me. I was sure teeth would follow. They didn't. Instead, he held me and rocked, shushing gently.

"Easy, my boy," he said as I struggled. His strong arms wrapped around me. I grabbed hold of the shadows and used them as whips to drive him away, and though he flinched at every strike, he was undeterred. He held me all the tighter and rubbed my back and my hair. "It's me, Tamil. All is well, Evan, I have you. Nothing will harm you here. You are safe. I am here."

Tamil. I knew him. He was the one who carried me. He gave me a bath and tickled my feet. I liked Tamil. I sobbed and buried my head in his chest as he held me close. He rocked me back and forth, humming a tune that I could hear in my ears, but could also sense in my soul as though there was another voice in harmony with his that reverberated from the very walls of the temple. Before long, I was fast asleep.

I woke again before the sun rose. It wasn't from bad dreams this time. Tamil was asleep in a chair in the corner of the room. I got out of bed and took my blanket. It was cold without a blanket. I climbed up in Tamil's lap and snuggled into his shoulder. I settled the blanket over us, because he looked cold, too. His arms wrapped around me as he cracked an eye and smiled. We went back to sleep.

The next morning, Tamil took me to meet a bunch of new people. I met Master Gregor. He cooked the food. There was a table that had big platters of meat, cheese and bread. Tamil said I could have as much as I wanted. Master Gregor laughed whenever I would come back for more.

"The boy's got a hollow leg," the burly cook said on my third trip to the table.

"It seems he does," Tamil replied.

"Well, stop by here before you leave." Master Gregor winked at me. I tried winking back, but I lost sight of him when both eyes closed. "I have a little something in the ovens that will be sure to top him off right."

Tamil smiled and promised that he would. So far, Master Gregor was my favorite. Well, other than Tamil, of course.

Master Ceridus squinted a lot. He squinted at his books as he made a notation and raked a pile of something into a box. He placed it on a shelf behind him while Tamil told him why we were there. He squinted at me and looked me over. He squinted at my hands, chest, and feet. He grunted and whirled about, the door banging against a wall in the back room. He returned a few minutes later with a bundle of clothes and a pair of boots on top. He started to hand them to me, but pulled away when I reached for them.

"On second thought…" He went to the back and returned with the bundle tucked inside a bag. "This way," he said to Tamil, "he can only soil one article."

"Probably a good idea," Tamil said, looking at the mess I had made of myself with the sweetcake that Master Gregor had given me.

We took the bag to my room and placed it on the bed, then we headed for what Tamil promised would be the last stop of the day.

The courtyard was an open expanse of ground covered in small gravel. It ran from the main gates to the Temple Sanctuary in an oval. There were five posts wrapped in rope and set into the ground in the northeast corner. Four paths split off in the cardinal directions with a fountain in the center. Each path was lined with all manner of plants, many of which were flowering. At the center of the fountain stood a statue of a woman. She was tall and beautiful. Her hair lay in a coil tucked high on her head with one loose strand caressing her cheek. She stood with arms outstretched, clutching a bouquet in one, and her other seemed to reach out to invite you in for a warm embrace. She wore a tunic that came to her knees and left one breast bare. Her bare feet lay within the shallow pool. One foot planted firm, the other bent, toes in the water.

I stopped and stared. I felt an urge to run to the woman, to wrap my arms around her knees. I couldn't move. There was a buzzing in my head and in my chest. I shook it to clear my thoughts, but the buzzing wouldn't go away.

"What is it, Evan?" Tamil asked at my side. "What's the matter?"

There came a sudden surge then, of what I couldn't say. I felt it all around and within me. Abruptly as it came on, the buzzing stopped and the overwhelming sense of familiarity passed like it had never happened.

I pointed at the statue. "Who is that?"

"That is Hessa," he said.

"She's pretty," I said.

Tamil smiled. "Yes, she is. It is comforting to know that one who loves us as she does awaits us at the end of our lives."

I scrunched my face.

Tamil knelt down beside me, and we looked at the statue together. "Hessa is the goddess of death and life, and this place is her Grand Temple. All here serve Her in some fashion." He swept a hand to include everyone.

"Priests?" I asked.

"Many are, yes. There are a number of Priests and Priestesses here at the temple, as well as those learning to be such. There is much more than that here, though."

"Like what?" I asked.

"I'll let Zai fill you in on the rest. We have to see him now."

"Who's that?"

"He's the Keeper. He leads the Grand Temple and the Order of Hessa."

"What does he keep?"

Tamil's eyes grew distant as he knelt there, one arm around my shoulders. "Dusty memories and old promises. Come," he said after a time. "He's expecting us."

We entered the building at the end of the courtyard. It was the largest at the Grand Temple. Inside was a small vestibule that opened into a sizable room. Rows of benches filled the sanctuary with a wide aisle down the center. The aisle ended at a stone table, behind which rested an unlit brazier, and behind the brazier stood five huge colored windows, each glowing as they streamed multicolored shafts of light into the sanctuary. The center window was a near exact replica of the statue in the fountain, only it was more than twice as tall. The woman in the glass glowed with the sun's light, and that sense of familiarity flitted across my mind and slid away again, lost among all the other novel sensations.

The other windows depicted scenes that I didn't really understand, but they were not less beautiful because of it. The entire room made me feel comfortably reverent. I felt at home here. It was a strange sensation, considering I had no memory beyond the previous night.

We entered a hall off of the main sanctuary, and Tamil opened the door and motioned me inside. I entered a waiting room, of sorts. There were a couple of chairs against one wall. A tall bookshelf filled with books lined another. Lanterns hung from hooks beside the window, and a door was set in the far wall, attended by a young man sitting at a desk. He wore gray robes tied with a white cord. He looked up from his work and smiled at us as we approached.

"Greetings, Magister. I will tell the Keeper you have arrived." He disappeared through the door behind him, then almost immediately waved for us to enter the office beyond.

The office was decorated in much the same way as the assistant's waiting area. The desk was larger, and the chairs were of excellent quality with padded leather seats and backs. The shelves held older books than those displayed outside, and small figurines and baubles sat deliberately between clusters of volumes. A tapestry hung on the wall opposite the window. It depicted a scene of battle. In the image, a woman wielded a sword against many opponents. A man, his back to hers, was likewise engaged. Whip-like black strands of power emanated from his hands and seemed to dance across the image.

"This must be the young man you told me about," came a voice from behind the desk. He rose and skirted its edge, coming to a stop near me and Tamil. He looked to be about fifty. He had long hair that fell to his shoulders, and his clean-shaven face gave him an air of confidence and authority. His pale eyes and warm smile spoke of compassion.

"It is," Tamil said.

I thrust my hand out. "I'm Evanar, Nice to meet you, sir."

The man took my forearm in his much larger hand. I could barely grasp his wrist. He knelt to one knee, coming to my level, and smiled. "Greetings, Evenar. I am Zaipheth Ren."

"The Keeper will be taking care of you while I am away," Tamil said hesitantly.

"Where are you going? Can I go?" I asked.

"I am afraid you can't. I work for the Emperor, and he lives far from here. Besides, I have much to do. You have much to do as well," he said. "I will come and see you as often as I can, though. You will stay here with the Keeper and learn with the other children."

"Am I going to be a Priest, too?" I asked.

"You can," the Keeper said, "though you don't have to. There are a number of things you could learn here. Here at the Grand Temple, we teach several skills depending on your aptitude and ability."

"Like what?" I asked.

"Well," the Keeper said, letting go of my arm, "we teach the Priests, as you have figured out. We also teach other spirit mages how to use their power safely and effectively. The spirit is the gift of Queen Hessa, and those who wield her magic fall under her Order."

"Can I learn to use this magic?" I asked, "that sounds fun."

"I think you can," Tamil said. "I don't know what kind yet, though, and you are too young to tell."

"You think he can?" Keeper Ren asked Tamil.

"Look for yourself," Tamil said.

Keeper Ren knelt down again and took my chin between his thumb and forefinger. He lifted my face to his, and when our eyes met, I felt a cool sensation spread into me from his fingers. He looked into my eyes, but he didn't focus on me. It seemed he was looking through me. I felt a stir within my chest, and the Keeper recoiled as though struck. He fell back on his haunches, his eyes wide, and he looked to Tamil in shock.

Neither said a word. Tamil had a smirk on his face that seemed to anger the Keeper. But when they looked back at me, they both seemed concerned. I stood, fists balled, ready to fight. Part of me felt attacked, yet another part knew I should behave. I struggled against the urge to lash out. I was so hungry. Shadows leaked from my eyes and mouth. I panted as my little chest heaved and stirred the wisps that wreathed my face.

The Keeper got back to his knees and held up his arms. "Peace, Evanar. I won't hurt you. No one will hurt you here." That was what Tamil had said last night. I slowly calmed, and the shadows went away. I wobbled, and Zaipheth Ren took me in his arms and hugged me.

I WAITED OUTSIDE WITH THE NICE PRIEST WHILE TAMIL ARGUED WITH THE Keeper. They had said they needed to talk. I sat in a chair beside the door to the office. I don't think they knew that I could hear them, even through the closed door. I could hear lots of things.

"You saw. I know you did. What was it?" Tamil asked.

"I don't know. There is something bound within the boy. Tied by spirit magic more complex than any I have ever seen."

"You know what this means."

"I know what *you* think it means," the Keeper said.

"You know it had to happen sooner or later," Tamil said.

"I know no such thing."

"You just make sure that when the time comes, you fulfill our bargain. You Keep your oath."

"Your time with the Emperor has made you cold, Tamil."

"My time with the Emperor has made me aware."

"But now?" the Keeper asked. "After all this time?"

"Bandit activity is on the rise. There are more attacks on travelers, including Guardians and Finders. There are strange dealings going on all over the Empire, and it is not just constrained to the Empire. Now is as good a time as any, old friend. These are dangerous times. I do not envy you, but it must be done. Just make sure you do it."

"I know my duty, Tamil. You worry about your own."

Tamil grunted and opened the door to the office. "Come, Evanar. Let's see about some dinner."

"I'm hungry," I said as he took my hand and we left through the sanctuary. "Tamil, what's a Guardian?"

"Finders and Guardians roam the countryside, traveling from village to city and back, all across the Empire, looking for those with the talent. Mages. Finders have a rare ability to see the talent in a person and tell what that talent is. They can also tell if someone is lying. Keeper Ren is a Finder. A Finder's Guardian is their bodyguard and companion. Together, they have another duty to watch for necromancy in any form and destroy it. It is an arduous task."

"Like the picture in the Keeper's office?"

"Just so. The Guardian in the tapestry was Temaria. Her Finder was Elam. They were the first of our kind."

"I want to be like Temaria. Can I be a Guardian?" I asked. Tamil smiled then. An expression flashed behind his eyes and vanished in an instant.

"Possibly. We don't know what your talents are. You are rather unique. We'll just have to wait and see."

The Bargain

For two years, from breakfast until supper, I played with the other boys and girls. In the evenings, we would gather in the dining hall and learn our letters and numbers. Uncle Zai, which was what I had taken to calling him, said that it would help us. He said that it would even help with learning the sword when it came time. I was skeptical, but Uncle Zai didn't lie, so it must be true.

We played hop-square and jumped a rope spun by two other children. Sometimes, we would play Finder and Guardian, where one would be the Guardian and would run through paths that smelled of flowers and manure to seek their Finder, who was 'lost in the wilds' and needed our aid. When we found them, we would team up and seek another. We would chase them through the winding paths, swerving between Priests and worshipers, splashing through fountains, and crashing through manicured hedges, until we found the filthy Bleeder hiding in the wild. We would tackle them and then they would become the Guardian and set off in search of their very own Finder. Those were my best days.

Tamil would come and visit every few months. He lived in the Capitol and helped the Emperor, but he didn't talk about that much. He brought me sweets and toys from the city, and I always shared them. He taught me things, things that he said I wouldn't learn at the Temple. He always made a game of it. Sometimes the lessons were just for me, and sometimes all the kids could join in. That was always fun.

Within a couple more years, my play time had been whittled away to near nothing. For four hours—every day mind you—we had to sit and listen to the Priests ramble on about the glories and beneficence of the Great Queen Hessa. The more I learned about this Hessa, the less I liked her. She was taking up a great deal of my playtime. What time she wasn't claiming for her own was hunted by the Masters. In cruel fashion, they stalked me and my friends before pouncing and sending us on one chore or other. Eventually, we had no place left to play. They found us, even in our most secure hiding spots, and made us carry water or firewood for the kitchens. It wasn't so terrible, though, because Master Gregor was nice and he always smiled and gave us warm pastries and sweetcakes that he made specifically to reward our 'dutiful assistance.'

Uncle Tamil came to visit once, and it wasn't fun. He brought people with him. There were two women and a man. One woman removed a drum from a cloth bag while the man tuned a lyre. They wrangled all the children into the dining hall and we pushed the tables and benches back against the walls. They had us gather in the middle, and the last woman paired us each up with a partner. I was paired with Clara.

"What are we doing here?" Yaren asked.

"Mistress Nala is here to teach you all to dance," Uncle Tamil announced to a room filled with moans and groans.

"It is a valuable skill," he said, "and one each of you should at least be familiar with."

"Not to mention, gentlemen, a man who can dance is popular with the ladies," another voice chimed in. That garnered a round of 'ewws.'

"Uncle Darius!" I rushed to the newcomer in the hall and wrapped my arms around his waist. He scruffed my head, and I swatted at his hand.

"Since when did you get popular with the ladies?" Aunt Lis said as she entered behind him. I hugged her, too and she scruffed my head as well. I pretended to bat her hand away, but I didn't mind it as much when it was Aunt Lis. She nudged me back toward the line of children facing off against one another.

"Now, children," Mistress Nala said, "take your partner's right hand."

"No way," I yelled. "She picks her nose with that hand."

"I do not!" Clara yelled. She thrust her fists onto cocked hips and glared at me.

"How young do you learn that pose?" Darius asked Lis. He received a glare of his own, which he returned with a smirk.

"Tamil is right. It is a valuable skill," Aunt Lis said, still glaring at Darius. "And it's not so bad. It's fun, really, once you get the hang of it." Her glare turned to a dare for her Guardian as she held out her hand. "Perhaps Guardian Darius would like to demonstrate this skill what made him so popular with the ladies."

Mistress Nala signaled the musicians, and they began to play. It was a lively song.

Lis stared her Guardian down. He flushed with embarrassment but took her hand, and off they went. We children scattered to the edges of the room as they pranced and twirled around the dining hall. They passed one another delicately, dipping and twirling to the melody and spinning all about the space. As reluctant as Uncle Darius seemed at first, he looked to be having fun.

I noticed Uncle Tamil whispering to Mistress Nala. I didn't know what he said, but they both had mischievous grins as Mistress Nala signaled the two musicians and the tune changed.

Darius and Lis circled one another, one arm extended and fingertips touching. They closed and suddenly spun away from one another. Lis spun under his arm and reached behind herself. Darius caught her hand and whipped her back into his arms. They twirled and repeated the process, with Darius escaping only to be caught and dragged back in. They continued this game of escape and capture until it grew in intensity as Mistress Nala started playing a haunting melody over her companions. When it seemed the music itself would explode, Darius grabbed Lis and tossed her into the air. She spun and spun. He caught her and held her as the music came to an abrupt end. They were both breathing hard.

Uncle Darius looked as though there was something terribly important he needed to say.

Aunt Lis looked as though she were about to bite him.

"When did you learn to dance?" Lis asked him between shallow pants.

"I. Um. I took lessons," he said as he sat her down and blushed. He released her and took a step back, bowed to her, then turned on his heel and left.

Lis smirked at his back as though she had won some great contest, or perhaps a battle. She still looked like she wanted to bite him, though.

Our dancing lessons weren't quite so exciting, but I guess they weren't as bad as I thought they would be. Mistress Nala, or another, came by several more times during my years at the temple. The students began looking forward to it. It seemed the older we got, the more fun we had.

THE TIME FINALLY CAME FOR SELECTION INTO OUR RESPECTIVE SCHOOLS. According to the Keeper, we were old enough for the Finders to read us properly, which he did himself. He separated everyone by classes of Guardian, Finder, Bloodmage, and Priest, using his magic to ensure accuracy of placement. The Masters of each school took charge of their students and ushered them from the sanctuary afterward. When the last student exited the sanctuary, I stood alone with the Keeper.

"Why?" I managed to say through gritted teeth. My hands balled into fists, and my muscles strained.

"This is why," Keeper Ren said, reaching out and waving his hand near my face.

I could see thin shadowy vapors leaking from my eyes and mouth and flicking at the Keeper's hand. I gasped and took a step back, and they dispersed in a rush.

"What is that?" I said and stomped around the room. It wasn't the first time it had happened. A couple of the Masters had even seen it, but when I questioned them about it, they seemed at as much a loss as I was.

"I don't know, but it appears to be brought on by strong emotion," Uncle Zai said. His tone was caring and concerned.

"It only happens when I'm angry," I said sullenly.

"That is because anger is easy, son. It is the quickest emotion. It doesn't surprise me that your power manifests when you are angry. It can be a powerful emotion, but burns too hot and too fast. Anger can be a tool for the use of magic, but it is fickle. You will only ever see the true potential of your power when it manifests from a place of love."

"I don't understand."

"You will, one day. I hope."

"And you have seen nothing like this?" I asked.

"Finders can do something similar, but it is something that is learned. It is focused, intentional." He held up his hand, and a thin, dark strand sprouted from his palm. It wove about like a snake nearly as long as my forearm. In a blink, it was gone.

"My shadows don't look like that," I said.

"The fact that you can see it at all means you are certainly a spirit mage. People without magic, even elemental mages, cannot see the soul. What type of mage you are remains to be seen. We just don't know enough."

"So what does this mean for me? Do I even get a say in all this?"

"Ultimately, it is your magic that will see to your path. The Goddess only knows where that will lead you."

"You have looked. You should know what I am to be. Isn't that what you do? You are a Finder after all."

"It is what I do, and I have tried to glean from you where your talents lie. But with you, it is not so simple. It is as though there is another you within you. This much I have told you. It has remained dormant since you arrived, secured within you by your own power, a power I cannot hope to unravel and would hesitate to do so if I could. We just don't know what will happen."

"So I am broken, is that it?" I asked.

"You're different, not broken," he said. "Hessa does nothing without a reason, even if she does not make those reasons clear to the likes of us."

"But you have your suspicions," I said.

"You've been talking to Tamil again. My Guardian needs to learn to keep his tongue behind his teeth."

I sat there in grumpy silence. Uncle Zai made sense, as much as I hated to admit it. My heart was set, however, and I wouldn't give up.

"What if I studied a little of everything?" I asked, hope filling me for the first time since the gathering. "That way, when we figure it out, I can continue with that. I can still learn to be a Guardian and train with the sword. And you even said that more knowledge is better than less."

Uncle Zai laughed. "Slow down, my boy. You may have a point." He gestured for me to sit on a bench and joined me. He sighed. "Tamil and I have been giving this a great deal of thought and discussion. While we cannot say with any certainty what you are, we are relatively confident of what you are not."

"What am I not, then?"

"You have exhibited no signs toward healing, nor have you shown any aptitude for being a Finder, regardless of these shadows of yours. They are too chaotic for you to be summoning them intentionally. And you would have to be doing it intentionally, for when a Finder does this, the 'shadow' you see is a portion of their own soul projected outside their body. It takes a great focus of will to push yourself from your own body. I know of only one who is not a Finder who can do it to some small degree, but it took years for him to master it, and still he is limited in what he can do with it."

He gave me a moment for that to sink in.

"So that leaves Guardian and Priest," I said.

"It does," he nodded. "So I will make you this bargain. You study both. Learn the ways of the Guardian, as well as the Priest. I will make the arrangements."

I jumped to my feet, excitement bubbling over. Uncle Zai became stern then.

"You will attend to both as though you wish to learn. You will not shun your studies in one because you prefer the other. I'll not have you shirking your sword training because you prefer the company of dusty old books."

I lunged toward him and wrapped my arms around his neck. He laughed and patted my back.

"Thank you, Uncle Zai. I will do my best, I promise."

"See that you do, my boy. Now hurry, Brenn is probably at the quartermaster drawing weapons and other gear. Don't be late. Afterward, see Master Gwynn. In the meantime, I will explain things to the Masters so they understand your situation."

"I will, thank you!" I turned and started running for the door. I was elated. I would get to train with the Guardians. If it meant that I would have to study with the Priests, too then so be it. I would have done anything to be a Guardian. I was feeling cheeky as I reached the door. I stopped and turned to the Keeper, who sat there on the bench, a warm smile on his face. "You know, you're not nearly as stodgy as Uncle Tamil says you are."

He raised a finger to his lips. "Don't tell him," he said. "I've had him fooled for years."

So, by the time I was fourteen, I had my very own sword. It was made of wood, but still, it was a sword. They gave some kids swords, others they gave books. I got both.

Arrival

For a year, every morning at dawn, I would sit in the Priest's lectures and daydream about the sword forms I would do that evening. In the evenings, I, along with the other boys and girls, would practice our scales for both offense and defense under the watchful eye of Master Guardian Brenn. Sometimes they would let us spar against each other or against one of the Masters. That was my favorite.

I was sore at first. Swinging a sword was hard, even a wooden one. I wagered that it was much easier to swing a real sword. The older kids got to practice with real swords, and it never looked like their arms and shoulders would fall off. Master Brenn said we could have real swords when we learned not to cut off our own legs.

Master Brenn was nice in a bulldog kind of way. I mean, he never said nice things, but he didn't swat us like some other Masters did when we trained with them. He always spouted off stuff like, 'Stay alert and stay alive,' and, 'Look for an opening,' or, 'Look for work.' We thought they were silly. He had a hundred sayings, and none of us was sure what he meant by any of them. Me and the other kids had great fun imitating him in the evenings after supper and chores. We would stand atop our bunks with a foot on the headboard and proclaim the silly sayings until we laughed so hard that one of the Masters would shush us and put us to bed, always with a warning that Master Brenn had better never hear us mocking him or it would be the ruin of us all. Now, though, I think Master Brenn did it on purpose, saying those things as he did. Those aphorisms have come to me in the heat of many a battle and have saved my life on more than one occasion.

During much of that tomfoolery, I was an eager participant. But I had made a bargain, and I aimed to live up to it. Uncle Zai would not tolerate negligence on my part, and I didn't want to discover the consequences.

Each night, I sat on the edge of my bed over a camp table I'd obtained from the quartermaster and read about the history, philosophy, and tenants of the Temple. I read the holy books and wondered, if we were all in the Order, even the Guardians, why this wasn't required for everyone. The Guardians, Finders, and Bloodmages all served Hessa. It seemed reasonable to me that all should know who they were serving.

The other trainees in my Guardian class had basic lessons in these matters, which they attended occasionally. In the afternoons, I would join the Guardians in practical application, while the Priests did the same for their work with ritual. I supposed if the other Guardians wished to know more, they could go to the archive and learn.

They didn't do this, at least as far as I knew. Most were practicing the sword or other skills taught by the Masters. I didn't blame them, really. Had I not been required to do the additional study, I would have been there with them instead of poring over the Novice Priest's texts. It was during this time of intense study, this discovery of the nature of the Priesthood, that I discovered that I actually enjoyed the work. I loved training to be a Guardian, and I still hoped that my power would finally manifest in that way. I also found, however, that the more I learned of the Priesthood, the less I resented having to do it.

I made a mental note to ask Master Gwynn about how I was to learn the practical side of my Priestly duties. It was important, and if I were to be diligent, then I needed to be thorough. It was only right.

I had to admit that my life was good, even with the added work. I was fed and happy and old enough to know that wasn't necessarily the norm for children in my circumstance. Many orphans, unlike me, had no one to look after them. Guardians and Finders travelled all over the Empire, and every so often, some would return to the temple bringing with them tales of the places they had been. Sometimes these were stories of renegade mages and bandit attacks. But they also told of life in the towns and cities that lay beyond the walls of the temple. They sometimes spoke of children living in the streets with no shelter and no promise of food. These children were constantly hungry. They were cold at night and had no other recourse than to forage in the gutters, or steal enough to eat, either from merchants, pedestrians, or each other, during the day. They never got enough. I felt bad for them, but what could I do? I was just thankful that I had what I did, and I hoped that one day I could help those others. I didn't know if that would be possible. I rarely left the temple, but perhaps someday I could help.

Everything changed about a year later.

The beginning was innocuous enough. I had become comfortable in my routine. It was past lunch, and I had finished my chores with Master Gregor and was making my way toward the practice yard, licking honey from my fingers.

A commotion at the front gates drew my attention. Three wagons were entering the temple courtyard. As they passed the always open gates, I started to see riders entering alongside the wagons. The first was a Finder. Even caked with dust from the road, his red- and black-paneled trail robes made him look mysterious and powerful. A Guardian rode up beside him and slapped his back. They dismounted, and the Guardian led their horses away.

The wagons rolled to a stop, and the dust from the small caravan settled over all in the courtyard. The commotion drew the attention of all on the temple grounds. I sneezed.

By the time the riders dismounted Keeper Ren had appeared and approached the leader of the group. The Guardian looked dangerous and imposing in his light armor of crossed leather bands and weapon harnesses, from which hung all manner of deadly implements. He had long hair tied at the nape of his neck, and a scar that ran along his jaw.

The two men did not attend to formal greetings, but immediately embraced. They hugged one another as long-lost friends, each patting the other on the back.

"Donovan," the Keeper said as he held the man out at arm's length. "How went the trip?"

"Oh you know." The Guardian grinned. "Normal road boredom until a moderately sized group of bandits hit us."

"Really?" the Keeper asked. "With Finders and Guardians present?" Donovan shook his head.

"They are getting bold, my friend. It seems to get worse every day. This time they had some hedge mage that thought he could take on the whole lot. It wasn't much of a fight. The Finders shut him down quick-fast, and we took care of the bandits in short order." The grizzled veteran Guardian sighed. "The rest of the trip was pretty boring, actually." Keeper Ren grinned.

"Here's to boring trips, Brother," he said with a sidelong glance to the wagons. "So, what do you bring me?"

Donovan turned to another Guardian. "Allain," he called, "release the hounds!"

Allain smiled and called for those in the wagons to disembark. They did so in twos and threes. When the first few climbed down, I realized the wagons were full of children. Many were close to my fifteen years, but there were some who were much younger. There were far more than I had thought initially. When the last had hopped from the wagon beds, there were at least thirty, all carrying bundles at their sides or on their backs. I stepped closer to get a better look.

"Zaipheth Ren," Donovan said with a formal bow, "the Celate of the Western Temple sends her regards and blessings, as well as her candidates, to the Grand Temple and trusts they will flourish under your expert guidance and tutelage."

Keeper Ren returned the formal bow and responded, "It is with humility and gratitude that I accept the responsibility of such an undertaking, and I vow to do my utmost to see and develop the potential the Celate has generously placed before me."

The two men smiled at the conclusion of the formality.

"Why so many, Donovan? And so young?" the Keeper asked. "We

don't usually get them until they are at the Apprentice level. When the Celate wrote me, she said it was getting bad. Where is she sending the rest?"

"It is bad, Zai," Donovan said with a slow shake of his head. "The Emperor has sent troops to the western borders to stop the incursions from Meningal that the Celate wrote you about. Between the two armies, they are making orphans faster than we can take them in." He waved at the group of children milling about as they were led away to find rooms and food. "These are not all from that bunch, but many are. This isn't the only group either. We had so many that we couldn't house or feed all of them for long. We sent caravans like this one to the Northern and Southern Temples. Hessa's tits, pardon the language, we even sent a dozen to the small Temple in the southern isles. These are the ones that the Celate identified as having potential for the talent. She said you thought it best they be taught here, far away from the problems that are plaguing their homes. Behind her hand, she told me to wish you luck and to look for more as she discovers them."

"I'll do that. We have room here. And we'll make more if needs be. My staff is putting them in rooms now, and Gregor has been making sweetcakes all morning. I think it will be fine."

Several strayed a bit from the wagons while awaiting accommodations. Others huddled close within the familiarity of their traveling companions.

One figure headed straight for me. She was a little taller than me with chestnut brown hair, and once she got closer, I saw she had hazel eyes that sparkled in the noonday sun.

"Hi," she said, extending a slender hand. I shook it. It was callused in the same places mine were from wielding my sword. She looked at me curiously. Well, not me exactly, but my sword. "You have a wooden sword? That's cute. They don't trust you with steel?" She grinned devilishly, if not in condescension. "We don't have wooden swords at the Western Temple. Oh," she said, "I'm Ivey. Nice to meet you."

Hessa's Hells

I fumed all the way to the training grounds. "Just who does she think she is," I mumbled as I stomped up the path. "Coming here and insulting the Temple, and me? 'That's cute.' Hmpf." The more I recalled of the few words she had said, the more they galled me. "The nerve. And what was this about the Western Temple not having wooden swords? How are they so special that they can go straight to steel swords? They're not better than us. I'll show her."

I barged into the training yard to see that the rest of the class was already there. So was Master Brenn. Every head turned toward me as I entered the circle. The other trainees shuffled around to make room.

"I hope we weren't keeping you from anything important, Hostric," Master Brenn said. That got some snickers from the other students.

"Sorry, Master. I was watching the new arrivals," I grumbled.

"Don't be sorry, be better. Early is on time, on time is late. Don't forget that. Now about these new trainees," he said. "The Western Temple has sent us this batch of promising new students. The class will grow some starting tomorrow. We need to see where they all fall out, therefore tomorrow is an assessment day to see where they rank."

"Shouldn't they already know where they rank?" asked Mallus from the other side of the circle.

"They should, and they'll be close," Master Brenn said. "Much of that is subjective, though. Normally we get new recruits from the other temples when they are already at the apprentice level. There is a minimum skill requirement to become an Apprentice, which is clearly defined."

"You have to be able to draw," spouted Alanis.

"Correct," replied Master Brenn. "With all the trouble out that way, though, the Western Temple is crowded, so the Keeper elected for them to be sent early. It will require some reshuffling on our part, but we can handle it."

"Why can't they just finish their training at another temple?" I asked, still fuming over the stupid girl and her stupid, sparkly eyes.

"Because all Guardians are trained here once they reach apprentice level. Same with Finders. It's easier to match you lot up that way." That raised surprised murmurs from everyone. "Some of the transfers are close to being able to use their power, whether they be Finder, Guardian, Bloodmage, or Priest. The ones that will fill this class will be Guardian Novices, who, like yourselves, are close to being able to draw."

"Wait, so we'll be standing around all day watching them test?" said Clara, who stood next to me.

"Oh, don't you worry about being bored," Master Brenn said. "You'll be testing, too. Some of you might move up to the next class tomorrow, depending on how well you boneheads have been paying attention. That's the whole point of this. You are all Novices now, but you do well enough tomorrow and you could move up to Initiate. Hessa's tits, you draw tomorrow and you'll see yourself an Apprentice."

The buzz of excitement was palpable. Most Novices moved up to Initiate when they were skilled enough. But if you drew, that was a guaranteed apprenticeship. Everyone knew that most Apprentices drew for the first time during an assessment. Assessments carried a lot of weight and a lot of pressure. That stress inspired a need for the draw and increased an Initiates chances at achieving the coveted ability. It was what we were all trying to do. It was the rite of passage. If we could draw, we could be Guardians.

"Alright, alright," Master Brenn said as he tried to regain order. "So that's what's going on tomorrow. Today will be light. We'll run through forms and scales, then you knuckleheads will go eat and rest for tomorrow's trials." That perked everyone up. An easy day was rare. I had a feeling tomorrow would make up for it.

The forms were easy, or should have been. Master Brenn would call out a maneuver, and we would execute it. He would yell parry, or riposte, or any other technique, and at each step he would evaluate our form, making subtle or even not-so-subtle, corrections to our positioning, and we would continue.

Sword scales were different. Scales were pre-planned, designed to anticipate the movements of our enemies or force them into positions we could exploit. They were named moves designed to be executed automatically. They were difficult, each containing three to eight movements, broken down into attack and defense. Master Brenn knew if we did one out of order.

We all lined up and began our easy day.

He may have intended it as an easy day, but the excitement of the upcoming activities was such that none could focus on their forms, and we all stayed there until everyone got them right. By the time I got back to the barracks, I was dripping sweat and bone tired. I entered the barracks room that I shared with nine other boys and stripped. I wrapped a bathing cloth around my waist and slid into the washroom. There were three other boys in there, and none spoke, which was a testament to Master Brenn's displeasure at our performance.

I bathed and dressed, deposited my clothes in my laundry bag for later cleaning, and donned fresh tunic and trousers. I even changed out my boots, as they, too, were soggy from the exertions of the session. I belted on my sword before I left. No Guardian would ever be caught dead without their sword, and though I wasn't a Guardian yet, it seemed like a prudent habit to form early. Besides, it was my sword.

As I made my way into the dining hall, I noticed that the room was packed. I had momentarily forgotten that thirty new kids had arrived.

That's not right, is it? I thought. *We are no longer children; we are Novices.* We had been all along, but now it seemed more real. Rationally, I knew I would eventually take part in an assessment. We all talked about it, wondering what it would be like and hoping we would draw and secure our places in the Guardians.

It was strange to think of yesterday in terms of being a kid, and today being a Novice at the Grand Temple of Hessa and training to be a Guardian. I had been here since I was six. This place was normal to me. It wasn't until I saw the looks of awe on the faces of the new arrivals that I realized how fortunate I was and how complacent I had become. I had grown so comfortable in my life that I had neglected the actual reason I was here. I shook my head at the realization, too tired to process it, and made my way to the line to get some food. I was tired enough that I would have even foregone the meal if my stomach wasn't convinced that my throat had been cut.

I felt a bump as I picked up my wooden trencher. The plate fell to the floor with an embarrassing clamor. I looked up to see one of the new students glaring at me from beneath a mop of sandy hair.

"Watch where you're going," he said and jostled me again as he brushed roughly past and picked my plate from the floor. I held out my hand to take it. In my fatigue-addled mind, I thought he picked it up to give it back. He hadn't. He looked at my outstretched hand and snorted. Then he looked me up and down and got an amused look on his face as he slapped my hand away. "Nice sword you got there," he said. "Your boyfriend get you that?" That garnered chuckles from his hangers-on and a few others within earshot.

My face was already red from drawing attention with the plate, but now I could feel the heat of anger rise to my cheeks. The boy was half a head taller than me. I took a step closer and gripped the hilt of my sword in warning. He laughed in my face.

"What are you gonna do, runt? Paddle me?" This brought on another round of laughter from his followers. I glanced around and saw that they were not the only ones who were watching. I spotted Ivey, who had stood for a better view alongside the rest in the dining hall. She looked as interested in the outcome as everyone else, though I saw a slight smirk on her face.

I'll show her, I thought, *I'm not afraid. We'll see who's better.* My eyes narrowed at her and I gave her a look that said, Watch and learn.'

That's when he hit me.

I sprawled backward into the table of plates, sending them scattering all over the floor of the dining hall and causing an uproar from the others in the room. The students scrambled to form the requisite circle around the combatants while chanting 'fight' over and over, as though we weren't trying to do just that.

I tried to recover, to spring to my feet and deliver this bully a lesson. I succeeded only in stumbling vaguely upright. As I took a lumbering step toward the shaggy bastard that sucker punched me, one of his lackeys tripped me and I fell, face first, into a rock-hard fist. It took me a second, during which Shaggy lifted his hands up to encourage the chant, to gain my feet again. I was wobbly, but I could still go. I advanced on him, but someone from the circle of onlookers shouted a warning and Shaggy spun with a powerful wide swing. I ducked under it and delivered a hard blow to his groin.

He doubled over and puked on the floor. When he rose, he had tears in his eyes. His face was a mask of pain and rage. Several of the others flinched and grumbled at my tactic. But Master Brenn taught us that there was no such thing as a fair fight. If you lived at the end, you won. If you died, you didn't have to worry about losing, so take the cheap shot. Shaggy was enraged. Everyone, including his lackeys, backed up a step at the look on his face.

He beat me bloody.

Blow after blow rained down upon me, and I took them. I had no choice, really, and I was seconds from unconsciousness when the bludgeoning suddenly stopped. I looked up through a rapidly swelling eye and saw Master Gregor holding Shaggy by his collar, his booted toes barely touching the floor. How he did it, I had no idea. Master Gregor had been the cook as long as I had been here. I had only ever considered him the cook, and a good one at that, but here he was holding a boy that was a half a head taller than me, and broader, on his toes. I realized then that 'Master' was not an honorary title.

"I don't give two tits what is happening tomorrow. A little time on the Hells will calm ye Right. The. Fuck. Down." He reached down with his free hand, grabbed my collar, and picked me up as though I was an afterthought. He dragged us both from his dining hall.

'THE HELLS,' OR HESSA'S HELLS TO BE PRECISE, WERE POSTS SET IN THE ground in the northeast corner of the courtyard. They stood four feet tall and wrapped in rope. The top of each tilted at a different angle and direction. The angle was so slight that it was difficult to tell which tilted which way until you were atop them. It was a punishment used by the Masters to instill discipline and enforce the rules of the Temple. I had been on each of them many times over the last few years, and this one was my least favorite. It tilted to the right, causing you to have to lean far to the left to maintain balance on the cursed pillar.

The fractious student would climb atop the post which was a foot across, and squat with one leg extended. They would then place their hands out to the sides, palms upward in penitence to the Goddess Queen for their transgressions. The students in question then had to listen as a Master lectured on the pertinent and not so pertinent lessons from the holy books regarding our offenses. Usually this went on for a half a mark, or even a full hour at most, but it seemed that any chaos in Master Gregor's dining hall inspired him to expound on the scriptures at length. Three hours we perched atop the Hells with a leg switch in between. The Master dared us to fall off, as he promised a whipping to beat the best we'd ever had.

"Dismissed," Master Gregor finally said. "And mind this when next you decide to fight in my dining hall." He walked away to his own quarters and called over his shoulder. "Don't you dare be late for the assessment."

I fell off of my own Hessa's Hell and landed on my back with a *woof*. I couldn't have climbed down. Shaggy did the same. I tried to move toward a sitting position and couldn't even do that. So I just lay there for a time, trying to recover. My eye had swollen completely shut by the time we had mounted the Hells. I felt with my hand and found swelling, but not as much as I'd had at the beginning of our punishment, and not nearly as much as I expected. My vision was clearing. Still on my back, I turned my head toward Shaggy to see him glaring at me. I struggled, but eventually rose. He followed suit. He looked as bad as I felt.

I limped over to him. He may have pummeled me half to death, but we survived the Hells together. Surely that counted for something. I extended my hand and cleared my throat.

"Good fight," I said.

He slapped my hand away like he had in the dining hall. He glared his hate at me before he turned and stalked off.

I could barely hobble as I crossed the courtyard toward my barracks to change and hopefully get a bit of sleep before the assessment the next day. It was after midnight as it was, so the 'next day' was relative, I supposed. The night air was humid, and the cicadas were loud in the late hour.

My entire body hurt. Every step through the courtyard sent spasms through muscles I didn't know I had. As I turned down one path for the short torturous walk to my barracks, I just knew that I would do miserably in the assessment. My body would stiffen the more I rested. I would have to stretch thoroughly before laying down, and when I woke, to even have a hope of walking to the training grounds at dawn. I had made it to within twenty paces of my barracks' door when Ivey slid up beside me. I straightened my back and tried to ignore my screaming muscles as I played off my hurt. There was no way I would give her the satisfaction of seeing me weak. She had seen me get beaten, so I was not sure why it bothered me. But it did, so I did my best to ignore the pain.

"Gorse," she said without preamble. I stuttered to a halt and turned to her. It took entirely too many movements.

"What?" I said incredulously to the nonsense she spouted. She shrugged.

"Gorse Larkin. That's his name. You know, the boy you got into a fight with?" she clarified. "He was an ass at the Western Temple, too. Everyone's afraid of him."

"I'm not."

She made to touch my swollen face and split lip but stopped herself. She winced. "Maybe you should be."

"He's a bully," I said.

"You won't be able to make him stop. He's too big, and he is a skilled fighter, as you have discovered. He also has too many friends licking at his boots to give you a fair shot."

"We'll see," was all I said. She shrugged.

"Have it your way, but don't say I didn't warn you," Ivey said. "Good luck in the assessment."

"You too."

We broke off there, with her heading toward her barracks and me to mine. In my pain and self-pity, I didn't notice the figure in the shadow until a familiar voice sounded low from the darkness.

"So," he said, "what did you learn?"

It was a familiar phrase. I had heard it often when I was younger, less so as I grew. Not that I made fewer mistakes the older I got. It was that as I grew, they expected me to perform this exercise on my own and without the prompting of my mentors.

The man who stepped from the darkness had asked me that question many times. It might have been my personal torment, but it was useful. It made me consider the things I had done, mostly mistakes, and examine them for what they were: lessons to be learned from and not repeated.

"Uncle Tamil," I said, startled but too tired to care at the moment. "When did you get here?"

He smiled. His teeth reflected the lantern light from the courtyard. "Answer the question, boy," he said. He wouldn't let me evade and I knew it.

"I learned I don't much like bullies," I said. He grunted in acknowledgement.

"What else?"

I brushed past him, my thoughts only for the minuscule amount of rest I would get before my assessment. "Fight, then gloat."

I heard his soft chuckle from the darkness as I shut the door firmly behind me.

Assessment

Despite Master Gregor's warning, I was late. The only thing that saved me was Alanis and his terrible balance, which he lost, and fell into my bunk, startling me awake. Mallus was the only one who seemed ready for the assessment. He was dressed, armed, and walking out the door before I even stood. A few of the others sped after him, tying on sword belts and fastening laces on their tunics. Even Alanis rushed out ahead of me, dressed and mostly ready, as I struggled into my trousers. I needed to hurry. I ran a hand through my hair which I noticed was getting a bit too long. I'd have to see about getting it cut.

But I only had it cut last week, I thought. And I called Gorse shaggy.

I jogged to catch up to my group, and my muscles were warming with the movement when I realized that I didn't hurt. I wasn't even tired. I slowed and raised a hand to my face and discovered that it wasn't sore. Not even tender to the touch. The cut on my lip had healed as well. I stumbled a step. There was no way I could have taken the punishment I took yesterday and come away from it unscathed. Not only did it appear I didn't have an even have a bruise, but by the time I had fully woken, I felt energized and uncommonly ready for this assessment. While I didn't understand how this could be, I was grateful.

The boys from my barracks trotted in a strung-out group. The assessment was being held in the upper training ground located on the northern side of the Temple Grounds against the outer wall. What part was not bordered by the wall was outlined in shin-high stones that formed an oval. We didn't practice here much. There were stands for observers, but everyone was on the field, though they kept outside the stones to avoid the ire of Master Guardian Brenn.

I was the last by several minutes. I hoped Master Gregor hadn't noticed. I slid in next to Ivey. She looked at me, and her eyes widened. "Wow, you look good," she said.

"You're pretty cute yourself," I replied with a cheeky grin.

"You know what I mean," she snarled. Her eyes narrowed.

"You blushed," I said, my smile becoming wider.

"I'm serious, Evan," she hissed under her breath. "You took a beating last night and you're none the worse for wear."

"No bruises?"

"None." Her eyes were wide in disbelief.

"I wonder how Shaggy's doing after I punched him in the kittens," I mused.

"Kittens?" she asked in confusion.

"What do you call them?" I asked and leaned forward expectantly. She blushed again.

"I don't have to call them anything," she said in a haughty tone and a jut of her chin.

What am I on about? I had thought she was cute since I first laid eyes on her, even if she was rude, but I would have never told her so. Not that she was cute, anyway. What was wrong with me? I couldn't think straight.

"You're pretty when you blush," I said before I could stop myself. "It makes your freckles stand out."

Ivey's face turned an even deeper shade of red as she blew out an exasperated breath and shoved me into Alanis, who responded with a surprised squeak and tumbled into Clara. Clara swatted him.

"All right! That's enough!" bellowed Master Brenn as he stepped out onto the field in front of the rows of students.

At the side of the gathering stood all the Masters, those from here at the Grand Temple and those from the Western Temple that had accompanied the students. Keeper Ren was present as well. He was content to stand back, talking with Uncle Tamil, and let the Masters perform their duties unhindered. Opposite the Guardians stood the students who were undergoing training to become Finders. Bloodmage and Priest trainees made up the last group.

For the Priests and Bloodmages, it was just a good show. For the Finders, however, it was much more. Those who advanced on assessment day were more likely to become Guardians, just as they would become Finders. This was a prime opportunity for a prospective Finder to see who they might end up being blood-bonded to. The blood bond was an intensely intimate ritual that connected the souls of the Finder to their Guardian. They carried it for the rest of their lives. Through it, they shared strength and will. It was said that through the bond, a Finder and Guardian could always find one another. It was rumored that the oldest pairs could share thoughts or strong emotions. The blood bond spurred each to protect and defend the other to the exclusion of all else. It was no wonder that prospective Finders would want to see what the next group of Guardians was like and vice versa. Regardless, to keep the students away from an assessment day could lead to a riot, and the Masters knew it.

"As of today," Master Brenn called out in his gruff parade ground voice, "there are no Western Temple and Grand Temple students." He looked to every one of us as he said this, making sure he drove home the point home. "From now on, there are Novices, Initiates, and Apprentices. All of you are striving to be Guardians. There is no room for division within the Order of Hessa."

"Where are the Apprentices?" whispered Ivey.

"They're on patrol with a few the Masters," I said. Ivey nodded her understanding. Master Brenn spoke up then.

"All students have been sorted into their appropriate skill levels, and we have randomly selected the names within each skill level that will spar one another. Each student will attempt to demonstrate their skill and prowess with the sword. We all know that other weapons are equally important, but none can argue that the skill with the sword will be your greatest asset in performing your duties should you be selected as a Guardian of the Order of Hessa. Each pair shall spar with training swords, and the bout will continue until three strikes are accrued and a winner is declared. The Masters will judge each Novice's skill and ability and agree on their ranking for the final selection in the classes. I extol each of you to perform at your highest level and warn you not to fight intending to kill or maim, though minor injuries are not unexpected. Violations of these instructions will be enforced by the Masters immediately and effectively. Do your utmost, and may Hessa guide your hand and heart as you compete today."

One of the new students raised his hand.

"Yes?" Master Brenn called on the young man.

"What happens if we do get injured, Master?" he said timidly. He was young and tall for his age. His voice only wavered a little when talking to the burly Guardian.

"Then the Apprentice Bloodmages have a fresh subject on which to hone their own skills," Master Brenn said, then chuckled. "I have no doubt they were just as attentive in their lessons as you were in your own." The Apprentice Bloodmages all looked a little gray at that announcement. Master Brenn waited a moment for questions, then motioned for another student to approach.

The student stepped up to him with a long scroll. He was an Initiate Priest, if I wasn't mistaken. I didn't know him, but I had seen him around the temple. He read off the first two names that would duel in the assessment.

The two made their way to the center of the field, each with their wooden practice swords. They both approached Brenn, and after a few words from the gruff Master Guardian, they were soon hacking away at each other. I leaned forward, watching the exchange eagerly.

The taller of the pair, Mallus, was from my own barracks. I had sparred against him many times and he was good. They'd paired him against a slight girl named Kathil whose strikes darted in like a viper and redirected at the last minute, causing him to have to change tactics and often abandon parries and counters to get his sword in front of her next attack. I was grinning like an idiot and bouncing on my toes in excitement. My heart beat in time with the clack of the wooden blades as they traded blow after blow.

"Are you well?" Ivey asked me. "You're acting strange."

"Oh yes," I purred, "I'm fine." A part of my brain, one I was actively ignoring, also noticed the difference. I should have been exhausted and barely able to walk after three hours on Hessa's Hells. But I found I was eager for the fight.

Mallus had apparently found his footing and was driving the Novice Guardian back step by step with a series of aggressive strikes. I could see his confidence return to him with each blow. He lunged in quickly to take advantage of a stumble. But it was a feint. The diminutive girl slid his blade just over her head and advanced quickly under the stroke to deliver a punch to his gut, and as she passed him, she brought her sword around to score a hard slash to Mal's hamstring.

The leg must have knotted with the blow, for Mal spilled forward and faceplanted in the dirt. Master Brenn called out a point as the boys from my barracks groaned in sympathy. The cry turned to shouts of discontent toward the young lady when she turned and struck again at Mal without waiting for him to recover. It seemed the students we faced this day had been trained with similar mentalities to those Master Brenn taught us. 'The fight isn't over when you have struck. It is over when your enemy is dead. A wounded enemy is much more dangerous than a dead one.' She continued her attack, not letting Mallus reset.

Mallus rolled and brought his sword around just in time to deflect. He kicked out and caught her squarely in the midsection. She rolled with the kick, but it was clear it had done its work as she struggled to gain her breath. Mallus leapt to seize the advantage, trying to employ the same tactics on her, but the knot in his hamstring hampered his stike She deflected the first blow. He countered and, knocking her swing wide, shouldered into her and opened her defenses enough to deliver a slash to her sword arm. Which earned him a point.

"She's good," I said to Ivey. "Are you all that good?" She shrugged. "Some are better, some not as good as Kathil."

"Where do you rank?" I asked, eager to know.

"We'll see," she said with a smile. "You had best hope we don't fight each other."

I reached out a hand and touched my finger to her cheek. She recoiled in surprise.

"What are you doing?" she demanded as she smacked my hand away from her face.

"Dimples."

"Well, you keep your hands to yourself," she said with a grin. The freckles that dusted her nose and checks flared more brightly against her reddening skin. "Are you all so unmannered here at the Grand Temple?"

I thought about that for a moment. She was right. I was behaving poorly. It wasn't conscious. I was acting without thinking. I would never behave like this normally. I had never done so in the past. Why should it be any different now?

I gave her a nod of apology and heard a cheer from the students of both temples. I turned my attention back and saw both standing with swords at their sides. Kathil cradled her left arm, and Mallus heavily favored his injured leg. He was also sporting a rapidly blackening eye that I wished I had seen him receive.

"What happened?" I asked Alanis.

"It was amazing," he said. "I've never seen anyone move like that. I'm not sure what happened, but Mal outdid himself. You can usually count on him being timid and cautious when sparring. He's been holding out."

"So Mal won?"

"Oh no," cried Alanis. "She trounced him good. He made her work for it, though. Oh, I hope whoever I have to fight isn't as good as her."

The next four bouts were much the same. The fighting was fierce, and I was gaining a new respect for the recruits sent by the Western Temple. I had to admit, their techniques might have been different, but their skill was every bit the equal of the Grand Temple students. The victories and losses proved evenly distributed.

From what I saw, the Western Temple fighters followed scales similar to our own. Where theirs differed was in the disengage portion of the scale. The way we were taught, there would be one to three attack forms, followed by one or two disengage. This would allow a breather to assess what we learned about our opponent and judge how best to continue. The Western Temple changed that by swapping a disengage form with an additional attack, to catch an opponent off guard. It was more aggressive, and I could see the benefit of it immediately. I resolved to talk to Ivey about it. If I could learn both techniques, it could prove advantageous.

The Initiate Priest announced Alanis next. Meri was about his height, if not shorter, with long black hair braided into a tail and hints of tattoos peeking from beneath the collar and sleeves of her belted tunic.

They were pretty evenly matched, with each scoring a hit early on. The rest of the fight was more tactical, but Alanis turned up the victor. I had to wonder if it was luck. He made it back to the line of students to back slaps and jeers. Everyone saw his performance and thought it was good, but it was clear that he had been sorely pressed until Meri stumbled slightly, leaving a gap in her advance that he capitalized on mercilessly. Meri stomped off the field, cursing a blue streak, angry that she let him get away. I had fought Alanis many times. She would have won, but for that slip. If I had to wager, I would bet she never made that mistake again.

The Initiate Priest stepped forward, and I snapped my head toward him at the sound of my name.

"... and Gorse Larkin," the Initiate finished. I grinned like an idiot and began bouncing on my toes again. My blood was up at the thought I would get the chance to get my hands on him. No, last night was not enough, as he had beaten me soundly. I was tired then. I was near exhaustion. Now, though? Now, even though I had only a couple hours of sleep, I was energized. I was buzzing with pent-up energy, and I was hungry. So very hungry.

I trotted out to Master Brenn, eager to begin.

My opponent was more subdued. While I had never laid eyes on him before our altercation in the dining hall, I could tell he was not walking with a natural gait. He moved as though he was stiff. Three hours on Hessa's Hells would do that. I wondered how effective my hit had been last night and how I could exploit it.

That annoying part of my brain still wondered why I wasn't sore, or bruised, or exhausted. I decided I didn't care why and would make the best of it. Ivey had said he was a good fighter. I wondered if I could make him angry to gain some advantage.

Shouldn't be too hard.

He finally made it to the center of the field. I gave him my best smile and kept bouncing. Master Brenn looked at me and narrowed his eyes, but he said nothing until we were both present.

"Remember, boys, no sword hits to the head, but fists and feet are fine. No strikes to the neck, spine, or groin. You will fight until three hits, with the sword, as called by me." Master Brenn said. I grinned even broader, not breaking eye contact with my opponent. "Questions?"

"Just one, Master," I said, still looking Gorse in the eye. "Hey there, Shaggy," I glanced down at his crotch. "How's the kids?"

The bully already had his sword in hand, while mine hung from an iron ring at my belt. He raised it against me, but Master Brenn gave him a sharp look. I merely leaned forward, daring him with a ravenous grin.

"Begin!" shouted Master Brenn and he backed away quickly.

I drew my sword and went on the offensive. One, two, three, four strikes I took at Shaggy. He barely managed to block them and gave ground in a panic. The sudden aggression of my advance nearly overwhelmed him. I was moving so fast that I couldn't believe it myself. I didn't feel taxed, either. I just wanted to hit him. I wanted to hurt him. I wanted his head.

That thought startled me, and I hesitated. I stood there, dumbfounded at my bloodlust. I wanted him dead, and I shouldn't have. I knew I shouldn't. I was as a practice dummy, sword held out, but not a true threat. It was all Shaggy needed to knock my sword wide and stab me in the chest. Master Brenn called a point. Shaggy immediately followed with a backhand across the face. That snapped me out of my torpor. He sent me reeling. I hit the ground with a thump, then tucked both legs and kept rolling out of the path of his follow-up. I was angry now. He would pay for that.

He overextended, and I dodged around him and caught him across the back with a cut and a point of my own, then followed up by hammering away at him until I knocked him off balance and stabbed him in the shoulder for a second point. He fell backward, but as he hit the ground, he threw a hand full of dirt into my face. It blinded me. He gained his feet while I swiped at my eyes to clear the debris. I could make out enough blurry motion to block the first two strikes, but as tears filled my eyes, he caught me hard with a solid slash to the ribs—and a loud crack.

Something within my chest tore. I thought it should have frightened me, but it didn't. Had he broken something inside me? I knew I had at least a cracked rib, but this was no rib I felt. This came from my core. It was a wash of heat and ice that filled my limbs and set my head and ears abuzz. I wasn't frightened, I was furious that I'd let him make me so vulnerable. I was also ravenous. I laughed.

We were tied at two points each, but I didn't care. I was no longer fighting to advance. I was no longer trying to win an assessment bout. I was here to hurt him.

He came at me again, and though I still couldn't see, I fended off every strike. During most of the exchange, my eyes were even closed as I tried to clean them, but it didn't seem to matter. He came at me with a thrust, and I guided it past me, within an inch, then spun up his arm and backhanded him across the face. He staggered and let fly a flurry of strikes that would have driven me back at any other time. This, however, was not that time. I blocked them all and even ducked under a wild swing to smash the pommel of my sword into his foot with a crunch. My laughter became mad giggles.

"Onsey twosey, rosey tosey," I sang the common children's verse.

The move caught him unprepared, high as he was off his recent success. He grunted in pain and hopped away. I followed and harassed him with every staggering step. I hadn't stabbed or cut him, so the blow didn't count as a hit and it did not end the match.

I cleared my vision, finally getting my eyes open, and fixed him with a hateful glare. His eyes widened in shock and surprise. It was time to have some fun.

He made a cut for my shoulder, and I stepped in to the swing and caught his wrist. I slammed my head square into his nose with a satisfying crunch and felt warm, sticky blood splatter my face. I pushed him away and made a show of licking my lips as I laughed madly.

The trap is sprung.

I almost felt as though I was no longer in control of my body, though I certainly was. I was merely being guided by something more than rational thought: pure instinct. I felt that control slip away as the instinct became more aggressive, more animalistic. I moved around him gracefully and delivered blow after blow, but never with the blade so as to not gain the final point and end the match. No. I had another agenda. And all the while, I laughed.

I punched him in the gut and drove the air from his lungs with a *whoosh*. When I pushed him away, Master Brenn caught him. He snatched the wooden blade from Shaggy's hand and placed himself between me and the and the bully turned prey.

"Get back, boy. He's drawing," Master Brenn said to Shaggy. "He's not looking to win now, he's looking to pay you back for last night, in trumps."

Shaggy stumbled away, leaving me only Master Brenn.

"Keeper," Brenn shouted. "His eyes aren't right. Have you ever seen the like?"

"I have not," the Keeper replied.

"Press him, Tomas, let's see what this is about," came Tamil's voice. It seemed eager and nearly as hungry as I was.

I looked at the burly Master holding the wooden practice sword. It looked like a toy in his meaty grip. He twirled it in a familiar gesture. It was all the invitation I needed.

Master Brenn was not moving slow like Shaggy had. He easily blocked my first few swings and punches. He delivered a few of his own, and while his fists and feet hurt, I found I could keep his sword from my flesh with little effort. I ramped up the pace. I was not dealing with a Novice, and I used every scale he'd taught me. We went at each other as though the fate of the world would be decided in this one fight.

The speed at which we fought was blinding, and I was just getting started. At least I thought I was until he ducked under a sword stroke and punched me in the gut. He followed up with a cut of his own, but I blocked it and delivered an elbow to his temple that staggered him.

"Enough, Hostric! Stand down!" Master Brenn shouted over my attacks. "This match is over."

I didn't stand down. In fact, my laughter increased with the speed of my attacks. Master Brenn matched me stroke for stroke. He never gave ground. Rather, he moved to the side, always toward my weak side, to lessen the strength and accuracy of my blows.

"I said stand down, boy!" he bellowed.

I did not.

I should have.

Master Brenn was my teacher. This was an assessment, wasn't it? It didn't feel like one. He took my prize from me. He took my prey. I would punish him for that.

No. That wasn't right. Master Brenn called the fight.

But the enemy isn't dead.

When I attacked next, I aimed a cut for his middle. Master Brenn backed out of reach faster than I could have ever guessed, parried, using a maneuver I had never seen before, and caught the back of my hand with the blunt edge of his sword. I felt bones break, and my sword went flying. I immediately felt my hand shift and reposition the damaged bone.

I should have stopped. I knew I should stop, but the pain was excruciating, and my anger was white hot. I lunged at Master Brenn, both hands extended. I would tear his throat out. A simple matter.

He sidestepped me casually, brought his iron-hard fist around to the side of my head, and swatted me from the air like a petulant bumblebee. I was out before I hit the ground.

Concession

I started awake with the sound of a lullaby and a door clicking shut. The room, if I had to guess, was in one of the Sanctuary wings of the main temple. There was a chair, a couple of unlit lamps and a window with the shutters open wide. The bright light illuminated a fuzzy image coming toward me. I rubbed at my face to clear my eyes.

"Hello there," a soft voice said. "You're safe, Evan. It's just me." The panic in my chest must have registered on my face. I sank back into the bed and released a pent up breath as Ivey crossed the room.

"What happened?" I asked as she pulled a chair close to the bed and sat in it.

"What happened?" She scoffed. "What happened was you drew. Master Brenn had a time putting you down, too. You cut him up good. He went off to the Bloodmages, and Master Donovan had to take over for him to finish up the assessment."

I was astonished. I thought hard, trying to remember what had happened. I knew I fought Shaggy in the assessment. Somehow, I ended up fighting Master Brenn? Yes. I remembered something along those lines. This was terrible. I didn't want to hurt anybody. Except for maybe Shaggy.

"What I remember is more than fuzzy, but I thought Master Brenn blocked all my cuts. Plus, we were using wooden swords."

"Maybe he did. I don't know. But wooden swords or no, at the speed you two were moving, you could have probably taken a head off with them." Ivey shook her head in astonishment. "You both were moving so fast, it was hard to tell. That's not the disturbing part, though. The disturbing part was the shadows. Even the Keeper said he had seen nothing like it. There were shadows whipping around you like live snakes, darting in and out. Every time one struck, a cut would appear on Master Brenn. He had a good fifteen or twenty bloody gashes by the time he finally knocked you senseless. It was scary."

I sank into the bed with my hands over my face as I moaned. I had screwed everything up. How could I have even hurt him? He was a Master Guardian. "What have I done?"

"Don't worry about it," Ivey said.

"How can I not worry about it?"

"You injured a Master Guardian the first time you drew. You'll be a legend. At least you didn't kill him," she said. "That would have been awkward. But that's why only Masters may oversee assessments, you know, in case a student draws for the first time and gets out of control. It happens fairly often, from what I've heard. When you draw for the first time, you don't know how to stop. Whatever it was you did, it was way beyond that, but still."

I appreciated her trying to soothe my guilt over hurting Master Brenn.

"My own experience wasn't nearly as dramatic," Ivey added with a smile.

"You drew?" I sat up in excitement. "Congratulations! We'll be Apprentices together."

Ivey's face flushed, and it was then that I noticed that my blankets had fallen from my chest and sat rather low on my lap. With this much of me exposed, I became more than aware that I wasn't wearing anything under the blanket. I quickly pulled the blanket to a more modest position as I settled against the headboard.

"I-I'm sorry about that," I stammered. "I didn't realize…"

"Now look who's blushing," she said with a crooked smile.

"Yeah, about that." I scratched my head in embarrassment. "What I said, right before the fight, I feel I should apologize to you. I never meant to embarrass you, and I don't want you to think poorly of me. We've only known each other a short time. I don't know what came over me, but I'm normally not like that."

"Like what?" she asked sweetly. She was pouring it on, and I felt my face flush to match her own.

"You know," I waved a hand as I floundered for words that wouldn't embarrass me more than I was already. It was a hopeless effort. "forward." She laughed and shook her head and I felt my skin grow even hotter. I couldn't hold her gaze any longer.

"You're cute when you're flustered," she said. "I mean, you face off against Gorse and practically take him apart, then you fight a Master Guardian and injure him, and not by accident. But let a girl call you on a compliment and you turn to mush." She sighed and shook her head slowly. "I swear, I will never understand boys."

"They weren't important," I mumbled.

"What?" Ivey asked. I looked back at her then, and she wore a confused look. I cleared my throat.

"They weren't important. They were enemies," I stammered, "at least at the time. Enemies aren't important, they are, well, enemies. I'm not concerned about their opinions because I intend to bash their heads in anyway. But girls, um, women I mean… You… You are important."

We both sat there in stunned silence. That moment. That moment, right there, was the conception of opportunity. We had a growing friendship already, but now? Now, I was terrified that I had revealed too much. I had told her how I felt. I didn't know if I was supposed to. What did I know about girls, anyway? I knew how to fight. I had the basics of the Priesthood. Apparently, I could draw. But I knew nothing about women. I broke out into a sweat, afraid that I had done something wrong, said too much, made myself too vulnerable. Even during my first fight with Shaggy in the dining hall, I wasn't this nervous.

I've messed everything up. Again!

"Do you mean it?" Ivey asked quietly.

I could have played dumb and ruined the moment, but even I, as profoundly inexperienced in such matters as I was, recognized the importance of my next words. It would define much of who I wanted to be. I could avoid the question. I could play it off as the effects of the drawing. I could do any number of things, but I found that what I could not do was lie to her. Not to her.

"Yes." I looked into hazel eyes set into a perfect, freckle-dusted face, and smiled. Whatever came of this, at least she knew. She looked at me for a long time. I would have given anything to know what she was thinking. I didn't look away. I dared not look away from those beautiful eyes. The centers were the color of rust that faded to pale green. I was utterly lost in them, and I barely registered that she had spoken.

"Good." She leaned down and kissed my cheek, then spun and headed for the door. She pulled it open and jumped back, startled. "Oh, Keeper. I'm sorry. Um, I—I was just leaving." Ivey took two steps back into the room and bowed low.

Uncle Zai chuckled. "I didn't mean to startle you, Ivey. How goes the training?"

Ivey blushed to her ears. I wondered if it was due to the attention of the Keeper, or being caught in here with me. Her freckles stood out on her reddened face and neck. "Very well, sir, thank you! I am honored by the opportunity to train at the Grand Temple, and I am excited about being selected as an Apprentice."

"Well, you earned it, and I think you will make a fine Guardian," the Keeper said. "It is time I address the new Apprentices, I think." He entered the room. "Speaking of which, how is our patient?"

"Him?" she said with a sassy grin for me. "I think he's faking it to get out of training." With a wink, she skipped from the room and shut the door behind her.

I groaned.

"She likes you," he said as I sat there with an idiotic grin on my face.

"If she liked me, she wouldn't have tossed me under the cart like that."

Zaipheth Ren sighed. "Oh my boy, you have much to learn about women and warriors. Lessons in either can be painful, but both at the same time?" He grinned mischievously. "Downright deadly. I pity and envy you all at once. What I wouldn't give to learn those lessons again for the first time." The Keeper's eyes lost focus, and he seemed to be elsewhere, either far away or long ago, or both. "Take some advice from a very old man. Enjoy this time. No matter what happens. It will feel as though it is the most wonderful experience that you could ever have. It will feel as though there could be nothing left worth living for. I assure you, both feelings are false. They are also, unfortunately, both true. Just try to understand that regardless of the pain, it is precious and irreplaceable."

"Sure," I said. I wasn't sure of anything though. The more I learned, the more I realized that there were far more people who seemed to know far more than I, and they didn't like the fact that they knew anything at all, which was doubly confusing.

"Anyway," Keeper Ren said, "how are you feeling?"

I thought about his question for a moment and then really examined myself for the first time since I woke. While I felt physically fine, I could come up with only one genuine answer. "Hungry," I said. I felt like I hadn't eaten in days. "How long was I out, Uncle?"

"A full day," he said. "The assessment was yesterday morning. It is noon the day after."

"I don't think I've ever slept that much," I said. The keeper shook his head.

"It's normal after your first draw. Besides, you took a solid punch from Brenn."

"How is Master Brenn?" I asked hastily. "Ivey said I hurt him somehow, though I don't know how I could. Something about cutting him, but I don't remember hitting him. I remember little, now that I think about it. And there were shadows?" I was rambling at this point. The words spilled out of me like a flood. I had so many questions.

"Easy, Son. He's fine. He stopped by to see you yesterday afternoon after he left the healers, against their orders, mind you. He wanted to check on you and make sure you were well." I sighed a breath of relief.

"I'm glad he's all right," I said. "But what happened? What was she talking about? What is this about shadows?"

"That's a very good question," Keeper Ren said as he looked me over. "I've been trying to figure that out myself. I've seen nothing like it. It was like when you were a boy and the nightmares came, but this was different. This was more deliberate, not wild and flailing like back then. The shadows seemed as weapons. You used them intentionally to support your fight with Brenn. And then there were your eyes."

"My eyes? They were gray, right? I drew, didn't I?"

"You drew all right, and then some," he said. "My boy, I don't know what happened. Your eyes were not gray, they were solid silver. When you drew, your speed and endurance both increased, shall we say, dramatically. Master Brenn had to draw deeply on his own talent just to keep up with you."

I rubbed the side of my head. There was no bruise and no pain, but I remembered the way he had batted me into the ground. "It didn't seem like he had much trouble to me," I said.

"You should have seen him," Uncle Zai said with a chuckle.

"And why am I not hurt? Did the Bloodmages heal me as well?"

"There was no need," Keeper Ren said with a shrug. "You were well on the road to healing yourself by the time we got you in here." Uncle Zai paused a moment before speaking again. "That's another thing. You shouldn't be able to do that. I heard about your fight with the Larkin boy. It was said that you got the short end of that. You then spent three hours on the Hells with Master Gregor. You should have been battered and sore, at the very least. You didn't seem to be. In fact, you looked to be in top physical order. I would suggest sending you to some classes with the Bloodmages, but even they can't heal themselves, so I doubt that will be of any help."

I sagged in to the bed. I thought my power had finally manifested, and I could become a Guardian as I had dreamed. But now, it was as if my drawing just made things worse.

"What's wrong with me?"

"I don't know that anything is wrong with you," he said, "but the shadows have me puzzled. Like I said, Finders can do similar, but the way you use them is different."

"I don't use them. I don't even know it's happening!"

"That's a problem, son. You know about the thing bound inside you. It is tied to your power, it is tied by your power. If I hadn't seen you heal yourself from the beatings you took from Larkin and Brenn, I wouldn't have pieced this together, but I have a working theory, which you will test with Master Gwynn. It is for this purpose that I am enrolling you as an Apprentice Priest."

"What? I don't want to be a Priest. I want to be a Guardian."

The Keeper raised his hands in a calming gesture. "I'm not saying that you cannot be a Guardian. I am saying that these other abilities are too strong to ignore. You require training, and I am uncertain even Master Gwynn can teach you, but he is the best option we have."

"So what's your theory?" I asked. I tried to keep the petulance from my voice while I heard him out. I wasn't sure I was successful.

"I can tell that what is bound inside you, is you. It is not foreign to you. It is as though a part of yourself has been torn free and bound with your spirit magic, and not by you. The magic is intricate."

"Like a Bleeder?" I asked in horror.

The Keeper winced. "To use a vulgar term, yes, and no. Those whose powers manifest in an uncontrolled environment are completely out of control. Their magic is torn open, and they leak, or 'bleed,' power. Yours was not torn open—it was removed, cut away clean, then bound, so as not to leak through."

"How? Why?" I asked.

"I do not know, but I suspect that this bound aspect of you is the source of your healing. I also think it was responsible for the shadows. The magic that binds it seems to restrain the shadows. That is what I see when I look into you. I believe that when you drew, you drew away power that restrains your other Aspect. Your speed and strength were much greater than we normally see in Guardians, especially young Guardians. Combine that with the fact that you healed yourself, and I would say you are likely to become the most powerful Guardian the Order has ever seen."

"Then the shadows are the problem?" I asked.

"Problem? No, not a problem. But it needs studied and observed. That is why you will continue with the Priests. Priestly power has to do with manipulating the soul. Your shadows, as we have been calling them, are not a mere trick of light and dark. I believe they are spirit. *Your* spirit. I am not certain, because I didn't get an opportunity during the fight to examine you. But there is a difference. I can use my power as a Finder to see another's soul and make assumptions based on what I see. I can use my spirit as a weapon to harm another's spirit. With enough damage to the soul, the body dies. I cannot use my spirit to harm another's body."

"I didn't know that," I said sheepishly.

"That is because you haven't completed your training. That is knowledge that you would not get through the Guardians, only the Finders and, to some extent the Priests. If your shadows are spirit, then they can affect the physical, not just the spiritual."

"I haven't even completed my Initiate's training. How am I to be an Apprentice to both the Guardians and the Priesthood?" I asked.

"The same way we would expect you to be an Apprentice Guardian without completing those studies: you work it out."

"What?" I cried.

"What did you think would happen?" Uncle Zai asked. "You drew as a Novice. The fact that you drew qualifies you for an Apprenticeship. Should I withhold that until you catch up on your training to ensure you have the requisite skills and knowledge?"

"I guess I didn't really think about it," I said. "I would assume you normally wouldn't hold me back, since I have always heard that if you draw, you become an Apprentice."

"You would be correct. The new Apprentice is responsible for catching up on whatever knowledge they missed out on. It is not insurmountable. So, you are offered the chance to complete your training with the Guardians, but you must also continue with the Priesthood."

"That's a lot of work," I sighed.

"It is. But you can do it." He sighed heavily then. "I can't believe I am going to do this, and if you ever tell anyone, I will deny it to my dying breath."

"What are you going to do?" I asked, suddenly wary.

"My Guardian and I do not see eye to eye on much," he said, "but if Tamil were here, he would say this, so I feel I must convey his sentiments on the matter. Verify with him if you think I am mistaken, but I know him better than anyone." The Keeper closed his eyes as though bracing for something unpleasant. "This is what you want, and this is what it will cost you to get it. How bad do you want it, boy?"

I smiled. "No. No, I don't think I need to check. It sounds exactly like something Uncle Tamil would say."

The Keeper smiled. "It's settled then. You rest. Continue your classes, both paths, on the morrow." I nodded my head in resignation.

"But first," he said, "we need to get you something to eat. The hunger that you feel results from drawing. Using your spirit takes from you. The soul strengthens you but leaves the body feeling weak afterward. The natural response to that is food, but food alone won't help. Rest helps, and a few other things, which you will learn in your apprenticeship. But for now you need to eat."

I smiled weakly at the Keeper, this man who raised me, and I saw the genuine affection in his eyes. I smiled.

"Thank you, Uncle." He nodded and scruffed my head before he left to find me a meal.

The Apprentice

The next morning, I dressed and made my way to breakfast. Though I'd had two plates of food the night before, I was still famished. I dressed in tunic and trousers and crossed the courtyard for the dining hall. The birds were loud this morning, and the rising sun on my face made me feel glad to be out of that room. As I entered the dining hall and made my way between the tables and benches, all talk in my immediate vicinity ceased. I saw a few familiar faces. I nodded and smiled. Their expressions were unreadable, and as I passed by each table, whispers resumed behind me. After getting a large plate of food, I spotted Ivey and made my way to her table.

"You finally get out of bed?" she asked playfully.

"I had to. I was going mad," I said. "I'm hoping some training will help sort me out."

"Well, it looks like you'll have to wait until the afternoon. Don't you switch classes with the Priests today?"

"Yes," I groaned. "Lessons with the Priests in the morning and training with the Guardians in the afternoon. I thought for sure that once I became an Apprentice, I could just train with the Guardians. I guess not much really changed. I'm still going to be doing both, just more of both. It's bad enough that I have to catch up on the Guardian lessons, but I have to do it with the Priests as well. I'll never sleep again with all the work I'll have just to keep up."

"Well, I'll help as much as I can," she said. "Hessa knows I could use the extra practice."

"Thank you," I said. "How goes it for you?"

Ivey sighed around a mouthful of bread. "I can't draw consistently. It's like I get close, then my focus slips and I lose it. Master Brenn said it will get easier. Master Donovan said to quit pissing about and do it already." We both laughed.

After breakfast, I made my way to the Sanctuary and found the class milling about outside a set of double doors at the back of the room. It seemed they were awaiting entrance. They all wore long gray robes with their hoods drawn back and waists tied with knotted cords. I was just as out of place here as the dining facility. The talking ceased as I entered, and all eyes were on me as I approached the group.

"Excuse me," I said to no one in particular. "I was wondering if this is where I needed to be. I'm—"

"We know who you are, Guardian Apprentice," said a voice from the middle of the group. A boy stepped forward. He was tall and about my age. "We all witnessed your duel." He proffered his hand in greeting. I took it. It was thin, but firm. "Welcome. I am Greymond Thewe, the student head. If you have questions, and I don't doubt you will, come to me. I'll be happy to help."

"Thank you, um… I'm sorry, I don't know how to address you," I said. "Would that be Apprentice Thewe?"

"He's polite," one boy whispered loudly. He was one of a trio that stood at the edge of the group.

"He's cute too. Even cuter up close," said the young lady beside him.

"Much cuter up close," said the boy to her left.

"He can also hear quite well," I said. I smiled at the trio, who blushed furiously and averted their eyes. I made my way to the group.

"Please, I am sorry if I embarrassed you. There is no need. I'm Evanar Hostric." I shook hands with each. They introduced themselves as Gauwen, Ellyn, and Ricio, respectively. The last two held on a tad longer than was necessary.

The door opened to reveal a man in the middle of his fifth decade. Master Priest Gwynn was head of the Priesthood within the Order of Hessa and Her Grand Temple. His dark hair and neatly trimmed beard showed the first signs of graying. His eyes were dark and full of obvious fondness as he looked upon his class. But they became unreadable when they fell on me.

"Come in, come in, let's get started," he said as everyone funneled around him and into the room beyond. I was at the edge of the group and the last to approach the large doors. The Priest stepped into my path, and I tried to gauge his intent with no success. I offered him a deep bow and introduced myself.

"Greetings, Master Gwynn. I was told to report for class." The Priest pursed his lips as he looked me up and down.

"You drew. I saw it. You should be an Apprentice Guardian." The Master crossed his arms and assessed me critically. "You shouldn't be here."

"On that, you and I agree, Master, yet here I am."

"*Why* are you here, boy?" he asked.

"I've been asking myself the same question. The long answer is that there is some question about my power that the Keeper wishes me to explore. He feels that the Priesthood is the best place to do that. The short answer is that I was told to come and learn, and thus I do."

"Is it that simple?" he asked. "You follow direction so blindly?"

"I trust the Keeper. The Masters are wise and impart their knowledge. It is by courtesy and respect that these relationships are upheld. That doesn't mean that I cannot or do not think for myself. Personally, I believe this is an enormous waste of time."

Master Gwynn waved away the statement. "Of course you respect us, we are Masters. We deserve respect."

"No, you don't."

Master Gwynn narrowed his eyes. Whether it was at being corrected or being included, I wasn't certain. That would have to be his problem. "I give courtesy because you are Masters and deserve such. I give my respect to those who earn it from me. My respect is mine," I said. "What is mine is no other's to command." He gave me a second look. He seemed intrigued.

"You are thoughtful and well spoken," he said. "But you are a bold one, aren't you? Not the usual type I get in my classes. Priestly types are generally softer."

"I have to be bold to be a Guardian," I said.

"But you are not here to be a Guardian, are you?"

"No, Master. I'm here to learn to be a Priest. After lunch, I'll go learn to be a Guardian." I sighed heavily. "Honestly, I don't know why I'm here. Keeper Ren apparently sees something in me, and for the life of me I can't discern what it is."

"Then there are at least two things that we agree on, Apprentice Hostric," Master Gwynn said. "Come, let's get you into some proper robes." Master Priest Gwynn then made for a smaller door set to the side and gestured for me to follow.

I emerged wearing gray robes tied with a cord of knotted white rope and carrying a bundle containing two more sets.

I returned to take my seat in what could only be loosely described as a classroom. The room was large, able to hold the small complement of students easily. There was little by way of decoration. Each of the students sat on a thin pad arranged around a central brazier. Every pallet was occupied but one. The Master Priest and I entered the room. Master Gwynn stepped between two students and sat cross-legged on the floor in front of the brazier. As he did, the one who introduced himself to me as Ricio turned to me and smiled and patted the pad next to him. I smiled back and took my seat.

Master Gwynn addressed the class. "I have been aware, since the events of the assessment, that Apprentice Hostric would join us. I have taken the time to speak with Master Guardian Brenn, not only about the young man but also to learn a bit about Guardian training. I thought it would be helpful in his transition."

Greymond Thewe raised his hand. "Forgive me, Master, I do not mean to question you, but I noticed you selected the white cord of the Apprentice for him. I find it hard to believe that he has mastered the skills of the Initiate and Novice and so deserves the title."

"You're quite right," Gwynn said. "Apprentice Hostric does not have the requisite skills and knowledge to pass the exams." The Priest looked at me then. "Do you, Apprentice Hostric?"

I held steady. I wasn't familiar with the politics within the Priesthood, but I was old enough to know there were politics within every structure of society, even down to the classroom. I decided to be honest and unapologetic. Let them do with that what they would. "I do not."

Greymond Thewe nodded in satisfaction. I continued.

"I am told, however, that by drawing, I have established a place for myself within the Guardians. I understand that there are similar contingencies in effect for the Priesthood as well?" I asked, looking at Master Gwynn.

He smiled and nodded. "There are. It is not common. In fact, I have only ever seen it once in my lifetime, but it is possible."

The other students looked to one another, stunned.

"By his own admission, Master, he does not have the skills required to perform at the level of Apprentice," said Greymond, "How will we be able to progress as a group when one will always hold us back?" Greymond gave me an apologetic look. "I'm sorry, Apprentice Hostric, I do not mean to insult you. I'm sure you can imagine what it would look like if any of us were dropped into a training session of the Guardians at a level beyond our capabilities."

"I would imagine you'd be injured quite severely," I said. "Even Novice training is dangerous for the Guardians." That brought a round of shivers and sage nods from the other students.

"I spoke with Master Brenn about this and learned some things," Master Gwynn said. "As you can imagine, the training regimens for the Priests and the Guardians are drastically different." He let that sink in. "Evanar, what do the Guardians do when one of their number is falling behind the rest in learning new skills?"

"We all teach them and help them until they are proficient, Master." That set the students to murmuring among themselves. "We believe that none are to be left behind, regardless of whether it is on a battlefield, isolated trail, or training ground. We look after one another. It builds the team and makes each member stronger."

"There is much, I think, that one may learn by studying disciplines other than one's own," Master Gwynn said. "If we do not challenge ourselves to learn more, to do better, then who are we and what good are we to those who seek Hessa's comfort?"

"What are you saying, Master?" asked Gauwen.

"I am saying that Evan has much to learn, and we have the information he needs. While it is rare for one to come to Apprenticeship within the Priesthood in such a way, it is not unheard of. We must devise a plan to help him succeed, or he will surely fail on his own."

I bristled at the plain statement, regardless of the truth behind it.

"Which is why," Master Gwynn said, taking in all the students in the circle, "you will all bring him up to speed." Groans and complaints sounded around the room, and I was struck at the difference between a class of Priests and a class of Guardians. The students in a Guardian class would have already identified a weakness in one of their own and developed a plan to help them. These Priests seemed appalled at the notion of taking on the extra burden.

"Ahem," Master Gwynn cleared his throat. That was another difference. Master Brenn would have been shouting by now. For the Guardians, it would have been a clearing of a throat. For the Priests, however, it seemed a harsh rebuke, for all fell silent.

"You say we are to teach him," Gauwen said after a pause, "but we're not Masters. We're not permitted to teach."

Master Gwynn raised an eyebrow. "Does it take a Master to impart the basics?" he asked. Again Master Priest Gwynn took in all the students before his eyes settled on me. "Do the Guardians not have a saying for such a thing, Apprentice Hostric?"

"A rising tide raises all ships," I said, quoting another of Master Brenn's limitless aphorisms.

The Priest smiled. "Indeed it does. By instructing Apprentice Hostric here, you will increase his knowledge and skill, and you will solidify your own competence. I believe the best way to ensure a sound foundation in your skills is to teach those skills to others. It will test your own knowledge and make you better Priests for the effort. Are you all not striving to become Masters in your own right? Is that not your purpose here? Because if it is not, I surely do not want you in my classes. It is my desire you all become Priests and Priestesses. When not actively involved with death rites and births, as the Goddess commands, the clergy is primarily teachers. A sermon is nothing less than instruction on the Queen's will, yes? What better way to develop these skills than as Apprentices training one another."

The students all looked thoughtful at the Master's words. Some nodded their heads in clear understanding, and others looked mortified at the prospect of having to work harder than they were used to in order to ensure the success of another. I didn't want to be here at all. I certainly didn't want to make other's lives more difficult for my benefit.

"I promise I will work hard to catch up," I said. The statement was lame, even to my ears. The other students must have thought the same, as some scowled when we began the first advanced lecture of my Priestly education. Master Gwynn did not back up in the lessons to fit me in, rather, he apparently continued from where he'd left off a previous lesson, and it left me feeling like I was alone on a tiny island with the tide on the rise.

IT TOOK TWO WEEKS TO GET THROUGH THE FIRST STACK OF BOOKS THAT Greymond and Ellyn had loaded me up with from the archives. All the of the Apprentice Priests were helpful. They were more than willing to explain difficult topics, or point it out if I had questions that would be answered in later topics. More often than not, however, they gave me lists of books to read.

I found that the more I read, the more I enjoyed it. There was a comfort in the books that I could not find on the practice field. Part of me wondered if I were becoming soft, but my afternoon training sessions with the Guardians disabused me of that notion. More and more, I was improving, both with the blade and with the scroll.

I returned a pile of books to the archive, retrieved another, and was headed to my room to store them before Guardian training. I took a meandering route through the temple gardens, as I used to do when I was younger. There was no place within these grounds that I was not familiar. I heard unusual noises coming from one of the outdoor shrines and took the next path to have a look.

The shrine was like many others that lay at the ends of the paths of fine gravel. A fountain lay in the center, with carefully tended beds of flowers encircling it. Several benches lay on the outer edge, and a small shed stood off to the side that held candles and other such paraphernalia for the conduct of personal rites and worship. Five boys stood in a semicircle around the front of the shed.

I made my way closer to see what all the fuss was about and as I neared, I could see Shaggy standing very close to the door of the shed, and between him and the door was a girl. She was younger than me and unlikely to have yet been selected into a particular school of study. I didn't know her, so she didn't grow up here like I did. She must have come in with the group that brought Shaggy and his minions.

"Hello," I said. "What's this? Am I missing something?" I asked. I knew full well what was going on. The girl had her face turned away and eyes closed while Shaggy leaned in close, his hand disappearing up the hem of her shirt.

I came closer and pushed two of the surrounding boys aside as I entered their circle. They didn't make a move against me this time. I guessed my display at the assessment was enough for them. Shaggy stopped his groping of the unwilling girl and faced me.

"This has nothing to do with you," he said. "Just mind your own business."

"It doesn't seem that the lady is very receptive to your advances," I said.

"She's receptive enough," he said. "I mean, she's an orphan. It's not like anybody cares." He laughed, which prompted a chuckle from his followers.

I went still.

"See, I'm not an orphan. I'm a noble. There are plenty of these wenches running around for the plucking. Maids, their daughters, nobody cares what happens to them."

"I'm an orphan," I said. "And I assure you I care."

Shaggy got red in the face. "You stay out of this. Don't you have Apprentice things to be about?"

"I do, but this seems awfully important of a sudden."

I moved closer to Shaggy, close enough to smell his breath. I extended my hand to the young lady, and she must have realized her only chance to escape him was with me. She took it. I maintained eye contact with Shaggy and backed away slowly, keeping her behind me. From my periphery, I noticed that his lackeys had not closed up the hole I made entering their little party and I backed toward it.

"You will regret getting involved in my business," Shaggy said.

"I doubt that," I said. "That would mean that I am concerned about you in some way. I am not."

"Not since you can draw, you mean."

I stepped closer to him now, leaving the young lady unattended for the moment to get in Gorse's face.

"If you want me, come have some. I won't even draw," I said. "But just you. Leave your friends behind." I stepped away quickly, pushing the young lady behind me. "Anytime, anywhere. Let me know."

I spun once I was out of Gorse's reach. "Don't do anything stupid, fellas. If any of you interfere, I *will d*raw, and I will beat every one of you within an inch of your lives," I said, then pointed at Gorse. "Starting with him." My threat was hollow. I didn't even know if I could draw again. I hadn't done it since the assessment over two weeks ago. They didn't know that, though.

I collected the girl and backed my way out of the circle. We made it to the path and toward more populated areas of the temple grounds. As soon as we stepped into the courtyard, she broke into tears.

"Are you alright?" I asked.

"I was so scared," she said. "Thank you."

"You're welcome," I said. "I hope you'll stay away from him in the future."

"Well away," she said.

"If you have any more problems out of him or his friends, please let me know." She nodded.

"What's your name?" I asked.

"Anna," she replied.

"A pleasure to meet you, Anna."

She smiled sweetly and went about her way. I knew I had already made an enemy of Shaggy. I wondered if I ignored him if he would just go away. I had more important things to worry about than him.

Training

I fastened the last buckle on my leather training armor and grabbed two wooden swords. I chuckled to myself when I remembered how much easier I thought the Apprentices had it not having to swing around these wooden monstrosities, and my delusion that the steel swords were lighter. The wooden swords were necessary today, though. Today would be more dynamic than an ordinary tutoring session.

I rushed to make it to the training ground. Having completed my training with the Priests that morning and lessons with the Guardians after lunch, I didn't want to be late for my sparring session with Ivey. She had been helping me make up for lost practice for some time now. I was grateful, but I knew that it helped her as much as it did me, as she was still having trouble drawing consistently. I aimed to help with that.

Ivey was waiting for me. I grinned thinking of how much better she wore the armor than I did. On me, it was practical. On her, however, it was so much more. Her hair was tied back in her customary braid to keep it out of the way and prevent an enemy from using it against her. When she saw me, her smile lit up her hazel eyes, as they glistened in the evening sun. I grinned back at her, knowing full well I looked like an idiot, but not caring one whit.

"For a moment I didn't think you were coming," she said. She noted the two wooden swords. "What is this? What are you on about, here?"

"I thought we would speed things up a bit," I said, tossing her a sword. "I think I got the hang of the new forms."

"What are you going to do with that? Paddle me with it?"

"Shaggy said the same thing," I said.

"Who? You mean Gorse?" she asked. "Well, you remember how that went for you, don't you?"

"Well, I can draw now and he can't," I said. "But you can." I pointed the tip of my wooden sword at her.

"Not well I can't." I knew it frustrated her, but I had come up with a plan. It was probably not a good plan, but it would be fun if she didn't kill me.

"While I'm practicing the advanced forms, you will practice your drawing. That's why I brought the wooden swords, so we don't kill each other."

"Oh, this should be fun." She loosened her sword belt holding her steel training sword and tossed it to the ground. "Come on then."

She came at me with an overhead strike that I deflected. The clack was loud in my ears, and it surprised me, having become so familiar to the ringing of steel blades. I stepped to the side and away from her attack to flank her, but she immediately pivoted, and her return stroke came for my throat. I danced back and out of the way, and she grinned at me.

"Those are basic forms," she said. "Aren't you supposed to be practicing your advanced forms?"

"Aren't you supposed to be drawing?" I asked. "The advanced forms are to be used when drawing. Tell you what. If you can draw," I grinned, "I'll use the advanced forms."

I saw her face go slack, a telltale sign that she was trying to draw. Master Brenn had explained that it was this intense focus that allowed a complete dismissal of our emotions as we fell into the meditation-like state that allowed our spirit to sing on its own. It wasn't how I did it, but apparently it worked for the rest of the Guardians.

Ivey and I exchanged several blows, punches, and kicks. I received one solid hit on my chest piece. The wide leather bands and the padding underneath absorbed the blow, but had she been using the steel sword instead of the wooden practice sword, I would not have gotten away with a mere bruise.

"You fight like my sister," I said—a verbal jab even as I followed it with one from my sword. She danced around both attacks nicely, thank you.

"Like you've got a sister, you motherless prick." She grinned as I jumped back and lowered my sword.

"Really? You had to go there?" I asked with mock hurt.

As we fought, each taunted the other. It was as common in sparring as in actual battle. There's a reason that soldiers are the best in the world at insults and jibes, for they know that if they can get under the skin of their enemy, they increase the chance of causing their opponents to make a mistake that could be exploited. Thus, the best technique for winning a fight, according to Master Brenn, was a strong arm, a quick tongue, and very thick skin. There is none better to practice with than a friend.

"Aww," she said, feigning concern. "Did I hurt your feelings? Want me to kiss it and make it better?"

I grinned wolfishly. "Would you?"

She sneered at me and attacked.

I dove under a left-to-right swipe and rolled, coming up behind her I swept my sword behind me using the same scale that Mallus had used during his assessment, but I aimed higher. It was supposed to be a hamstring cut. If it had been, she would have blocked it. At the last moment, though, I twisted my wrist, and instead of the clack against wood that she expected, there sounded a loud, meaty smack followed by a yelp as the flat of my blade struck her backside. I spun to a standing position, preparing to deflect a follow up blow, only to see her standing there looking at me with the most incredulous look on her face.

Her eyes were wide in surprise, and her mouth hung open, though no words came out. She just stood there, total disbelief writ across her face as she rubbed her stinging rear.

"Did you just?" she sputtered. "You didn't!" By now the fight was forgotten, and she stood in shock. "You bastard!"

I blew her a kiss. "Want me to kiss that and make it better?" I waggled my eyebrows at her. She blushed furiously. Then her eyes glazed over, and the sparkle of rust-green iris was replaced with the swirling gray film of a fully manifested Guardian in deep draw.

That was when the rules changed, and the fight started.

I had to draw deep as well to fend off the flurry of strikes as she came at me. Every move she made was technically perfect. She was using the advanced forms that Master Brenn had taught us. That meant I had to use them, or she would hand me my head. These forms were designed to take advantage of a Guardian's increased strength and speed. Ivey spun and whirled at one point, holding her sword tight to her body to defend, then sending it out in a deadly arc that I had to recognize and counter. Her sword was a blur. We danced around one another and traded blows, some connecting, some not, depending on the reaction and reflex of the other. Before she drew, I had been toying with her. But now that she was drawing, she moved with speed and grace which I was hard-pressed to match. Yes, I could draw faster and more consistently than her, but she was so much better with a blade than I was. I relied on my draw to be faster than my opponent. Since Ivey struggled so hard to draw at will, she focused her efforts on perfecting the forms. She made every move with perfect accuracy and economy of movement. She backed me up several steps and I was barely able to keep her from taking my head off.

Suddenly Ivey's attack shifted, and I saw an opening. I moved from defense to offense, and that was my mistake. I thrust at her middle, and she spun, grabbed my arm and dragged me past her. Off balance, I stumbled, and there was a loud crack as she brought the flat of her own weapon against my backside. I spun in surprise and tried to rub the sting away.

"Oh, that's how this is going to play, now is it?" I asked with a grin. She blew me a kiss this time and resumed her attack.

We fought not as though our lives depended on it, but something far more precious: our dignity.

We dodged, jabbed, kicked, and punched each other as we tried to paddle the other's rump with the flats of our swords.

While we had adjusted the rules of our sparring match, we were still employing the techniques that Master Brenn has taught us. We had to. It was the only way to defend ourselves and our increasingly tender posteriors. It amazed me at the speed at which we moved. The clack of the wooden blades as we cut and parried came closer and closer with each pass until the sound rolled from us like that of distant thunder.

At one point, she backhanded me across the face with her off-hand and split my lip. Sending me into a backward roll, I rolled one extra time, rising out of her reach. I snapped a kick that caught her in the chest as she charged me. She fell to her back with a *whuff* then rolled to her side, expecting my follow-up attack. She was not wrong. As she spun back to her feet, she swept my legs from under me and came down on top, straddling my hips to pin me down and pressing her blade against my throat.

"I surrender," I said and released my draw. I patted her on the shoulder three times, to acknowledge my defeat. She relaxed, and the smoky gray film covering her eyes faded away as though blown by a breeze, revealing those hazel irises that I fell into more and more often. She leaned down and kissed me softly, and I raised my head toward hers, wanting more. She responded, our breath coming quicker. The taste of her mouth and the smell of her sweat seared themselves into my mind. I couldn't forget that kiss if I tried. And I have tried.

When finally she pulled away, she bit my lip, the one she had split with her knuckles. I jerked away so quickly that I slammed my head into the ground. I saw stars and heard her grunt in satisfaction.

"Ow! What was that for?" I asked. She grinned, my blood smearing her lips like the paints some women wore.

"That's what you get for paddling me," she said.

I smiled, accepting my punishment, and strongly considered acting out more often if that was the consequence.

"I think I got the worst of it," I said. I raised my hips and ground them into hers, rubbing at my rapidly forming bruises. Her eyes narrowed in pleasure, then flew wide as she scrambled off me, her face burning crimson. She fell back on her rear and yelped in pain, then scrambled to her knees, her heels propping her up gingerly. We both fell into a fit of laughter.

"Ugh, I am a solid bruise." She rubbed lightly at her rear.

"Let's see," I said, leaning far over as though I could actually see.

"You wish!" she said, her blush deepening.

"Oh, yeah." I got serious then. "You drew. You drew quickly," I said.

She nodded. "I had something strong to focus on."

"What would that be?"

"Murdering you!"

I leaned forward and kissed her again. In the days and weeks that followed, we kissed often. We did a lot of things often.

The Enemy At Your Back

Many nights saw me awake in my room, hunched over my small desk with my candle and some tome or another. Tonight was one of those nights. The book I was studying discussed the very founding of the Order of Hessa and the war that brought it about. It speculated on the necessity of the Order and suggested its true purposes. I couldn't say that I disagreed with it, but I found my mind filling in blanks left by the text itself. It spoke of battles and the victors, yet there were no details of the battles themselves. I was daydreaming, even though it was the middle of the night. Necromancers and the newly founded Order of Hessa battled at the foot of Mount Haras, located somewhere in what would eventually become the Western Province of the Arulean Empire.

Finders and Guardians faced what the book called 'The Lost.' They were creations of necromancers that were more abomination than anything else. One spot in the text described The Lost as bodies of men brought to life with the souls of beasts. A true abuse of Hessa's gifts, both of spirit and of power, The Lost sowed chaos across the land and were the fodder that heralded more terrifying, more sacrilegious nightmares.

My mind wandered over the desperation that the Order must have felt as they fought these monsters out of their darkest fears. I imagined battles fought between these forces and sensed the ebb and flow of the war that would decide the fate of all mankind. As I did, I noticed the room flicker, the light incongruent with the flame from the lone candle that rested on my desk. Forms swirled and danced along the walls. Shadowy figures swung enormous blades and monsters beyond belief devoured soldier and Priest alike.

I gaped at the images on every wall of my tiny room and gawked. As though caught involved in something they ought not, they froze, then dispersed, back to whatever corner would hide them until ready for battle once more.

I rubbed my tired eyes, convinced that I had been awake too long, snuffed the candle, and turned in. Tomorrow was going to be a long day.

I YAWNED SO HARD MY EARS POPPED. IT TOOK ME A MOMENT TO REALIZE the Quartermaster was talking to me.

"I'm sorry, Master Ceridus. What was that?" I asked.

"What's the matter with you, boy? Are you getting enough sleep?" he asked. Master Ceridus's face was stuck in a perpetual squint.

"I don't think I've ever gotten enough sleep, Master," I said. "I was up late studying."

"That's right. You are the one who is working through both the Priesthood and the Guardians. Good thing you are wearing robes today instead of the armor," he grinned. "It would make for an uncomfortable ride, I think." He shrugged. "What were you studying?"

"*Essays on Order and Duty,*" I said. "The one written by Telleran Serai."

"Oh, he had some interesting ideas," Master Ceridus said. "It was considered quite inflammatory in its day."

"You know Serai's writings?" I asked. The surprise must have shown on my face, as the quartermaster chuckled.

"I wasn't always handing out swords and belts, young man. I was a Priest once, a good one too, if I do so say so."

"I mean no disrespect, Master, but how did you wind up as Quartermaster?"

He pointed to his face. "In case you haven't noticed, boy, I can't see worth a damn. Too many late nights hunched over books and parchments with naught but a candle." He shrugged. "For my reward of dilligence, I am nearly blind in one eye and can't hear a thing with the other." He laughed loud at his own joke. "Seriously, Son. Don't end up like me. Use two candles on your desk, or better yet, when you get back from getting my supplies, remind me and I will give you a lantern for your room. It helps."

"Thank you, Master Ceridus. I appreciate it," I said. "Are these the only things you need from the city?" I asked, holding up the note he had given me.

"That's all," he said. "And make sure you count everything. That bastard at the warehouse has shorted me in the past. The butcher you can trust, but count anyway. Don't let him think you lazy."

"Yes, Master," I said as I left his office and climbed into the clapboard wagon. With a flick of the reigns and cluck, I was around the storehouse, through the courtyard, and past the temple gates.

I had made this trip several times in the last few months. At first it was with Master Ceridus, as he had introduced me to the people and places that I would have to see to get supplies. Lately, I had been doing it on my own. It was a concession, as we all had duties to the Temple. Since I trained with the Guardians and the Priesthood, I had little time for the daily chores I had been doing. A trip into Drada every few days took longer, but was easier for me to schedule around. I enjoyed it, especially when the weather was like it was today.

The trees that lined both sides of the road were tall and cast everything in a calm, almost surreal light. Shafts of sunlight dotted the lane as they found their ways through the leaves. The Grand Temple sat on an island south of the port city of Drada. The island was connected to the mainland by a land bridge that was a mile long and wide enough for two wagons to pass abreast. It was said to have been created by earth mages after the war that saw the establishment of the Order of Hessa as a precaution to keep Her most sacred Temple safe.

As the wagon rumbled off the causeway, I entered a large intersection. A signpost pointed to Drada to the west, the Coast Road to the east, and Corinthia straight ahead to the north. Corinthia was the Imperial Capitol and where Uncle Tamil lived. As Magister of the Realm, he advised the Emperor and took care of 'a number of tasks on the Emperor's behalf,' whatever that meant. Eagerly anticipating the butcher's cured sausages, I pulled the wagon west and was soon entering Drada's warehouse district.

We finished loading the last of the supplies, and I drove the wagon to the butcher. I pulled the wagon behind the shop for loading, then walked around and entered through the front. A large counter made a square of one corner of the shop, Sizeable portions of smoked and seasoned meat hung from hooks, and the room smelled of the spices and smoke used to preserve them. The butcher was a tall, thin man with a genuine smile and a true talent for sausage.

He saw me enter and waved me over enthusiastically. "Evan, my boy. Come here. I want you to try something." As I approached the counter, he took his cleaver and trimmed off a piece of cured meat about the width of my thumb and tossed it to me. "See what you think of that. It's a new recipe."

I bit into the chunk, and my eyes widened in shock. "This is the best yet."

He nodded in obvious pride. "I'll send some back with you. You give some to the Finders and Guardians that come in. If this little venture works, every pair will stop in to get some on their way through. Once word gets out to the surrounding towns, I won't be able to make it fast enough."

I chuckled at his enthusiasm. He was always looking for a way to expand his business. As I finished the morsel, I wondered if this would be the thing to do it. "You might be onto something."

"You got the list?" he asked. I passed it to him. "Give me a minute and we'll get you loaded."

Between the two of us and his apprentice, it didn't take long. The apprentice scurried back inside and the butcher passed me a small sack.

"Here you go, Son. You make sure you give some to the Finders and such as they travel in. Don't keep them all to yourself."

"I promise," I said and shook his hand. He shut the back door of the shop, and I turned and set the sack on the floorboard beneath the wagon seat, pleased to have a snack for the ride home.

As I bent over the wagon, I felt all the air rush from my lungs at once. It was as though I had been punched in back. Someone grabbed the back of my head and slammed my face into the wagon.

I had been stabbed. I couldn't move as they kept pressure on the blade and a fistful of my hair. They leaned down, and I smelled a wash of putrid breath hit my face as a man said in a low, rough voice, "Larkin told me to say hello." Then the pain hit as he twisted the knife and withdrew it with a jerk. I still couldn't breathe or cry out. I wanted to scream, my back seemed aflame. He let go of me and I slid to the ground, half under the wagon.

I felt hot, wet blood run down my skin and fill my lungs. I couldn't take in air. It felt as though someone were standing on my chest. My thoughts were a jumble as I struggled to move. Through the fog of fear and panic, I heard a clear voice—a memory of one of the first lessons with Master Brenn after I became an Apprentice. In my head, he was screaming, 'When in doubt, draw!'

I did, and the power came fast, eager. Energy coursed through my body, and my back arched as my torn muscles reacted to the flood. Uncle Zai had said that I healed myself when I drew that first time, but I didn't know how to do it. My head cleared as panic fled the rush of power and my mind righted itself. I hoped that just drawing would start the healing, otherwise I would die here.

I could feel my organs begin to knit behind my ribs. Blood filled my mouth and throat. I tried to roll to my side to expel it and hopefully take a breath without drowning. I forced some from my mouth, then gasped, sucking blood back down my throat. I must have gotten a little air with it, because I went into a fit of coughing and vomited. I forced myself to all fours and heaved blood and bile into the alley.

By the time I could breathe some, I was weak, but still alive. I was still drawing, afraid to stop. Would the healing stop if I released the draw? I didn't know. Gorse. He had done this, or one of his sycophants. The more I thought about it, on my hands and knees in an alley puking up my own blood, the more enraged I became. The aggression that came from my unnatural draw only added to it, and I clawed my way up the side of the wagon and into the driver's seat. By the time I had the wagon headed out of Drada, I could more easily tolerate the movement. I could feel the skin closing on my back, but I had to lean over occasionally and vomit more blood as my insides tied themselves back together.

I continued drawing all the way to the temple. The trip took longer than normal, and night had fallen by the time I entered the temple grounds. No one was around. I parked the wagon by the storehouse and left it. I would deal with that tomorrow. Now, however, I had something to attend to.

I stalked to his barracks. The first two rooms I tried were empty. In the third, I found him and five of his cronies. Two were laying down, the other three were sitting in chairs playing cards over a low table. Everybody jumped up when I slammed the door open. I stood there with eyes glowing solid silver and covered in dark, tacky blood.

The two closest to the door came at me immediately. One swung a fist, while the other drew a knife. I punched the first one hard in the face, and he went down and stayed there.

"I told you what I would do if you got your friends involved, you shaggy bastard," I said.

The sight of the knife pissed me off, and I couldn't help but wonder if that was the one they'd used. It didn't matter. Even if it was, it was a tool. The hand wielding the tool stood on the other side of the room and had pulled his own blade.

That's fine.

I dodged around a thrust and grabbed his lackey's knife hand at the wrist. I brought my elbow around and took him in the temple. He crumpled. I stalked toward the object of my ire.

"Next time you want me dead, you come do it yourself, you coward," I snarled as I took down another of his pals. The last raised his sword and with draw-enhanced speed, I batted it aside and gave him two quick punches to the gut, then threw him toward the wall.

"Fine," I heard as Shaggy swiped at me with the knife. He attacked while I dealt with his friend, and I couldn't move fast enough. If I hadn't been drawing so deeply, he would have gotten me good. As it was, I jerked backward, and the knife cut a thin line across my cheek. I smacked the knife from his hand on his next attack, and it clattered harmlessly to the floor. I grabbed him by the throat and squeezed.

His eyes bulged, and he clawed at my wrists and hands to free himself. It would have been so easy to break his neck. I ached to kill him.

"No," I said as I loosened my hold enough for him to breathe. "I have a better idea."

I fulfilled my promise and beat him within an inch of his life. I pummeled him like he pummeled me the day we met. I left him lying there. He was still conscious. His nose and jaw were broken. One eye was filling with blood. I felt ribs crack when I hit him.

I stood over him as he moaned piteously, but I had none for him.

"When you go to the Bloodmages to get patched up," I said, hate spewing from my mouth as I leaned over him, "you tell them the truth. You tell them I did this. Then you tell them why. I will back up your story."

I staggered to my room. Too tired to hold the draw any longer, and reasonably sure I wasn't dying, I released it and was instantly exhausted. I fell across my bed into sleep's waiting arms, caught by the familiar, comforting melody of a lullaby.

Bonds of Blood and Love

I woke to a slam of my door and a rustle of fabric. I rolled from my bed, drawing as I did, and rose to catch my assailant by the throat. I lifted the man from the ground then got a good look at him. I dropped him immediately, along with my draw, and pulled him into a hug.

"Uncle Zai. I'm so sorry, I could have killed you."

He returned my hug then pushed me away to look at me. "What happened to you? You didn't make it back last night. When you didn't show for lessons this morning, Master Gwynn sent Ellyn to check on you."

"I came and knocked," Ellyn said, "and when you didn't answer, I tried the latch. It was open, so I came in. I saw you lying there like that," she gestured at me, still wearing blood-caked clothes. "I thought you were dead, and I ran to get the Keeper. It turns out you are not dead, you only look dead. Why do you look dead, Evan?" The more Ellyn spoke, the more heated and flushed she became.

"Because I should be," I said. "Someone tried to kill me last night."

"What happened?" the Keeper asked. There was a sharp edge to his voice and hardness in his eyes I had not seen from him before.

"Gorse Larkin. Someone stabbed me as I was leaving the butcher's, said that shaggy prick sent him. He left me drowning in my own blood in the alley. It turns out you were right, Uncle, I heal when I draw. It was the only thing that saved me. I am still sore, and hungry as all the hells, but I'm alive."

Ellyn turned pale white and gasped. Then her face reddened again, as if in anger.

"What then?"

"Then I went to have words with him and his friends," I said. "It was an interesting conversation."

"Did you kill him?" the Keeper asked.

"No," I said. "They were alive when I left them."

"I believe you, but I have to know." Keeper Ren raised a hand to cup the side of my face and asked me again. "Did you kill them?"

"No."

I understood his need to verify. I had something extremely violent and aggressive living inside me, after all. It would have been irresponsible of him to allow something like that to roam the temple unchecked. I restrained my instinctive reaction to lash out when I felt the cool power wash over me. I knew he wasn't trying to harm me, and I didn't want to hurt him.

"No. You didn't kill them," he said after a moment. "But Sweet Queen, you wanted to." He released my face and sighed. "I am impressed by your restraint." He regarded me for a moment, then turned. "Ellyn, do you know Master Guardian Brenn?"

"Yes sir," she said. "He's the big grumpy puppy."

The Keeper chuckled. "Yes, well, don't call him that to his face. You'll make him blush and he'll never forgive you." Ellyn smiled sweetly.

"Go fetch him for me, if you please."

"Yes, Keeper," she said, then stalked toward me. The diminutive woman reached out and punched me in the gut. "You scared me. Don't do that." She had tears in her eyes. Then she realized what she had done. Her eyes went wide with shock, and her hands flew to her mouth, then she looked at them. She had blood on her knuckles from my clothes. "Eww." She looked around for something to wipe her hand and, finding nothing, picked the cleanest spot on my tunic. She gave me a dirty look and stormed off to complete her task.

Within a few minutes, Master Brenn arrived, Ellyn in tow.

"Tomas," the Keeper said, "get Larkin and his friends and bring them to my office." He glanced to me and continued, "Take them to the healers first if they need it."

"Your little Priestess found me as I was looking for you," Brenn said. "I was coming to tell you they're gone. Their room looks like a battlefield. There's blood and almost all the furniture is broken. Their gear is missing. It looks like they took their things and left." He paused a moment, looking me over. "You look like you might know a thing or two about that, Hostric."

"I know a little," I said.

Master Brenn pointed at my bloody clothes. "Who does all that belong to?"

"Me, unfortunately."

Master Brenn grunted. "Then you suck and we need to step up your training."

"In my defense, Master, I had just been stabbed," I said.

"You don't look too stabbed to me," he said. "Save your excuses for success. Failure deserves better." He turned and left.

"Get some rest and clean up," the Keeper said.

"Need some help with that?" Ellyn asked cheerily. When both myself and the Keeper looked at her, she blushed but kept my eyes. "Just to make sure the wounds are clean, of course."

I smiled. "I'll manage, Ellyn. Thank you."

She gave a shrug that said, 'Your loss,' and with a quick glance at the Keeper, she bounced out as well.

Uncle Zai gave me a questioning look. "Her too?"

"Um. Yeah."

"Does Ivey know?" he asked.

"Apparently they are friends," I said.

The Keeper shut his eyes tight and pinched the bridge of his nose. "Good luck, Son."

I DID AS THE KEEPER SUGGESTED AND BATHED. I CLEANED MY ROOM AND replaced my bed linens and straw then dressed in my Priest robes and headed to the dining hall for lunch. I made it partway through my second plate of food, intentionally slowing to not rush through it, when I felt someone approach. I looked up to see a young man. I say young, because I was probably three years older than him at sixteen. He stood, hands in front of his waist, worrying the hem of his tunic. He wore a thick leather belt from which a wooden sword hung in an iron loop. I wondered if I looked that small when I was in his shoes.

I smiled at him. It was obvious that he was nervous. "Hi," I said. "Can I help you with something?"

He squirmed and looked at his feet. He glanced sidelong to a nearby table where his friends were looking to him in support. He straightened his back and faced at me. "I—um, well, we wanted to thank you."

"I can't imagine what for, I said. In my confusion, I nearly missed Ivey sitting down next to me.

"Well, we heard you ran Larkin off," he said shyly. "And we wanted to thank you."

"You heard about that already?" I asked in amazement.

"Even I heard about it. Ellyn told me about this morning," Ivey said with a raised eyebrow that promised that I would be giving her a full account later.

"I take it Shaggy was giving you trouble?" I asked the Novice Guardian.

"Oh yes. All of us. It was terrible. He threatened to beat us if we said anything." He then glanced at a girl at the neighboring table who dropped her head. "And worse."

"What is your name, Guardian?"

"Oh, I'm just a Novice," he blurted.

"Just because you don't have a Finder doesn't make you less of a Guardian. Start being one now, and you will have less to learn later."

The young man beamed. "That's what Master Brenn said when he taught us once."

"Master Brenn says a lot of things. You listen to him, it'll save your life."

"I am Aiden, Apprentice Hostric."

"Well met, Aiden. How about you and your friends join us for lunch?"

Aiden looked appalled then. "Oh, we couldn't."

"Why not?" I asked, then narrowed my eyes at Ivey. "Did you put up the 'No Eating with Apprentices' sign again?"

"Not me," she said with a smile.

We got up and went to sit with the Novices. By the end of lunch, they were much less afraid of talking to us and much more excited when we agreed to help them in their sparring for a couple of hours on their days off. It wasn't much work on our parts, to be honest, and they really seemed motivated. They were most grateful that Shaggy was gone. It seemed every one of them had some story that made me glad I had done what I did. Though I found myself wishing he hadn't left so I could do it again.

"You should have killed him," Ivey said as we left the dining facility. "You know what Brenn says about leaving an enemy at your back."

"I know. I couldn't."

"Why not?" she asked, her brows scrunched.

"Because I wanted to so badly. It felt wrong. In that moment I didn't know, or care, if he deserved it. All I knew was that I wanted it. It was wrong."

"Knowing him, you'll end up regretting it," she said.

We left the dining hall and made our way toward the courtyard, talking and joking.

"Hi, Evan." came a voice from edge of the yard.

"Oh, hi, Anna," I replied with a wave and a smile.

"Have a fan club now, do you?" Ivey asked with raised brow.

"Well, you know," I started, "when you have it like that, you have it like that."

She punched me.

All sound was suddenly drowned out as a horse, lathered and laboring, skidded to a halt in the central courtyard carrying two people. Rock and gravel sprayed out in front of the manic animal. The beast's eyes were wild as they rolled in its head. It stamped its feet and shifted from side to side in sheer panic.

The rider in the rear wore banded leather armor that crossed in front of his chest.

A Guardian, I thought.

His scabbard was empty, and he teetered precariously in the saddle. He swung his leg over the back of the horse, and when his foot touched the ground, his leg buckled and he fell to his back in the gravel.

The one left atop the horse swayed, and I drew. I arrived just in time to catch the lithe figure as she toppled. She was wrapped in a cloak. Through the dirt, mud, and blood that covered them both from head to foot, I recognized the man. Guardian Darius. But that meant... As I lowered the Finder to the ground, the hood of her cloak fell back to reveal a familiar face.

"Aunt Lis!" I cried.

I looked around, and though there were others making their way to us, they were too slow. "Ivey, get the Keeper." She whirled and sprinted off. "And a Bloodmage!"

I removed the clasp and opened Lis's cloak. Blood covered her neck and chest, so much so that I couldn't see the wound. I started feeling for it and I found a broken crossbow shaft protruding a finger's width from her tunic, just above her breast. This was beyond me. I had the basic medical training with the Bloodmages that all Guardians received, but I couldn't deal with something like this. Her eyes fluttered and closed.

"No!" I screamed. "No, Aunt Lis!" I slapped at her face, and her eyes flew wide. I looked up searching frantically, and after only a few moments I saw Keeper Ren and Master Jaerun running headlong toward us.

"Hang in there, Aunt Lis, help is coming. The Keeper and Jaerun are here."

I eased Finder Lis's head to the ground and skittered backward quickly as the Keeper slid to the woman's side.

No, Blessed Mother, not Lis, I prayed frantically. My studies with the Priests took over in my impotence. Master Jaerun grabbed the Keeper's shoulder and bodily threw him backward as he fell to his knees over Lis. I could feel his magic reaching out before he even arrived, such was his haste.

Keeper Ren scrambled from his back to crawl over to the Guardian. No. Not the Guardian, Darius. Lis's Guardian. Uncle Darius was frantically trying to claw his way to Lis's side, his hand searching for his missing sword, to defend her. He was maddened. His eyes searched all around, seeking enemies where there was none. He looked nearly dead himself. His instinct and the blood bond he shared with Lis were the only things keeping him sane, driving him to protect her. He could feel she was dying, and he would do anything, kill anyone, to prevent it.

Keeper Ren grasped the man, slid behind him, and dragged the delirious Guardian back against his own chest. He fell into the Keeper's lap, his face full of sorrow, but not the mad panic of a moment before.

"Lis," Guardian Darius sobbed.

"Easy, Son," Uncle Zai said. "She's in good hands. She will be well. You made it."

Tears streamed down the Guardian's blood-smeared face as he watched Master Jaerun tend to his Finder.

Darius closed his eyes and began to pray, "Blessed Queen, Beloved Goddess, take me instead. If you must have one, let it be me. I vow to serve any post, perform any task, fulfill any oath, just please take me instead." He fell into silent sobs as the Keeper held him.

"She'll be all right, Darius. Jaerun is tending to her. You remember Jaerun?" Keeper Ren said gently. "Tell me what happened, Son."

"They ambushed us on the road," came the hoarse answer. "Arrows." Darius coughed, his injuries catching up to him. "Lis's horse died where it stood. It fell on her, and she took an arrow to the chest. I dove off my horse to help her, and that's when they attacked." Darius went into another coughing fit.

"There were dozens of them. I fought them off until they retreated to get their crossbows back up. I pulled Lis from under her horse and threw her on mine and we ran like Mikos himself was after us." His breathing was becoming shallow and thready.

"Shh," the Keeper said. "Catch your breath, Son." Then he turned to me. "Brenn." I turned on my heel and ran.

I found Master Brenn as he exited the dining hall. "Master Brenn, come quick! The Keeper called for you. There's been an attack. It's Lis and Darius." I turned and ran, not even checking to see if he followed. He did. In fact, he streaked past me, his eyes gray stormclouds and and his breathing unlabored.

We arrived back in the courtyard, and Master Brenn ground to a halt, quickly taking in the scene.

"Ambush," Uncle Zai said. "Large force with ranged weapons. Find them, but do not engage. Track them if you can."

Brenn nodded.

The Keeper turned to Darius. "How far, Darius?" He got no response. The Guardian's mouth opened, but no sound came out. His eyes were focused on Lis and Master Jaerun. Master Jaerun had been pouring power into Lis's still form since he'd arrived. His skin was pale, and the air was thick with magic. Jaerun's breathing was labored, and Lis's chest barely moved—but it moved.

"Show me, Darius. How far?" The Keeper slapped the Guardian's face to bring him around. Darius held up his hand, fingers splayed, before it collapsed back to his lap.

"Five miles beyond the causeway. Scout ten in an arc. Report back. There is something happening out there, and I want to know what it is. Defend yourselves if necessary, but avoid contact. They are becoming bolder by the day."

Master Brenn nodded and headed toward the barracks. In minutes he, along with a half dozen Guardians and senior Apprentices, sped out the gate on horseback. I would likely have been with him, were it not for my trials last night. I cursed that I couldn't help track down those who had done this.

I heard a gasp and saw Master Jaerun collapse across Lis's still form.

The Keeper looked to me, fear and dread on his face. "Get more healers."

I brought two more Bloodmages, and by the time they finished their work, both Lis and Darius were unconscious, as was Master Jaerun and one other healer. We got them into rooms off a wing in the sanctuary. We put Lis and Darius in the same room that I recovered in after I drew for the first time. A team of Apprentice Bloodmages, under the watchful eye of a Master, tended to them.

I stood by the Keeper, out of the way, and watched as they bustled about the room ensuring everything was just so. Zaipheth Ren stood stone still and his eyes were hard and cold.

"There was a time," the Keeper said, his voice a barely audible whisper. "just after Simian's War when Finders and Guardians were feared, and for good reason. We walked the continent, confident in our power and the right of our cause. We hunted dark practitioners like animals and executed them publicly and without mercy. Our methods were…extreme, and the people feared us, feared what would happen if we found our quarry living among them. There was nowhere they could they hide." He paused for a long moment. "If I find those responsible for this, I will remind them what it is to fear. Aside from lore, I am also the Keeper of Oaths, and this I swear."

Iela

It was three days before Aunt Lis woke, and another two before she could get out of bed on her own. Darius never left her side. I laughed my entire walk through the sanctuary wing when Lis told him to go buy a new sword or something and quit mothering her. It was a half-hearted jibe, and he knew it. Something had changed between them, but I decided it wasn't any of my business. So I sought Master Gwynn.

I entered the sanctuary and found Ellyn replacing spent candles and removing wax from the polished wooden racks that held the daily devotions of the Order's faithful, of which there were many. This was the Grand Temple, after all.

Ellyn saw me enter, and her face brightened. "Evan," she said, "you're early." The diminutive blonde twirled the end of her shoulder-length hair. Even though she was friends with Ivey, and knew how close Ivey and I were, I didn't think she had completely given up. Not quite, anyway.

"Hi, Ellyn," I said. "I need to see Master Gwynn. Is he in?"

Ellyn nodded. "Yes, he is. Just knock first." She placed the back of one hand along the side of her mouth and faux whispered, "He might be taking a nap. He does that a lot."

I chuckled. I had always adored her perky exuberance. Her constant good mood was contagious.

I smiled, offered my thanks, and proceeded to the classroom at the back of the sanctuary.

I knocked on the door and heard a muffled 'come in' from the other side.

Master Gwynn leaned over to blow out a candle that sat at the corner of his desk and made his way toward me.

"I'm sorry to bother you, Master," I said.

"You are not bothering me, but I do have someplace to be."

"Well, I found myself with some time and was hoping to get some extra study in," I said and fell into step beside him.

His brows rose at that. "How does someone neck deep in two difficult disciplines find himself with time on his hands?" he asked. We exited the sanctuary and I followed him along a winding path.

"I, um, had some issues, and it required me to use a great deal of power a few days ago. I am nearly recovered. I could probably go back to training with the Guardians, but I would rather not press it."

"I heard of your 'issue,' and you were lucky to survive it," Gwynn said. "But you have pressed your power before. It is like exercising a muscle—The more you use it, the stronger it becomes. Have you had problems from doing this which are causing you such difficulty now?"

"I have to some extent. It becomes hard to control myself and not hurt those I am sparring with. If you recall, I have mentioned to you before that my power differs from the other Guardians."

"Well, you said your eyes were silver, where theirs are gray," Master Gwynn said.

I nodded. "Yes. Keeper Ren thinks maybe I am stronger than other Guardians, potentially, at any rate. He believes that perhaps the closer to silver our eyes become, the more powerful we are." I hesitated. "It's more than that, though. The more power I use, the more aggressive I become. There are other emotions, too. Those scare me more. I don't want to hurt people, Master Gwynn."

"Isn't that the mandate of the Guardian? To protect your Finder at the cost of having to hurt people if necessary?"

"Yes, but the more aggressive I become, the more I want to hurt people. And the less it matters who."

"I see," Master Gwynn hummed. "I admire your concern. There are few who would exercise such caution. Very well. You may study with me today, then. I have to admit that I have been curious how your power would fit with the Priesthood. Now is as good a time as any to find out. This way, I can evaluate you."

"I haven't had to use much power in my studies so far. Will this be any different?"

"No. Most Priestly duties require little raw power. That was why I was so curious about you. I have never known of a Guardian becoming a Priest. I know that their power only affects their own spirit, but you are different. You have been able to perform all the rituals with little to no effort."

"From what I can tell, the purpose of much of the ritual is to establish focus to access your power. That's the first thing we are taught once we learn to draw."

"An astute observation. How to the Guardians teach that level of focus?"

"Usually Master Brenn hits us with a wooden sword until we figure it out," I said.

Master Gwynn chuckled. "I believe that if I adopted that technique to forego the rituals, I would end up with Apprentices in tears. No, the old ways work for us. I think we will stick with our rituals, for now at least."

I smiled at the thought of Master Gwynn swatting students with a practice sword and yelling at them to clear their minds.

"We are here. Are you ready to for your first practical application as a Priest?"

We were standing outside one of the larger shrines reserved for the Priesthood. I had played in all the shrines as a child, but I had never been allowed inside one when the Priests were actively using them.

"What will we be doing?" I asked, looking curiously at the small stone structure.

"We are delivering a baby."

I felt sweat break from my skin in cold rivulets. "We're what?"

"You heard me. You have been studying with us for a long time. You know what we do."

"The texts say that we assist in death and birth rituals. It didn't say we delivered babies! Oh Hessa, we don't execute people too do we?"

"Calm down, boy," Gwynn said. "We assist in the child's birth and assure a smooth transition of the soul from the Goddess to the child, through the mother. And we don't execute people. We perform death rituals to ease the suffering of the dying and send their souls back to the Queen, feeding Her and the well of power from which the Order gains their strength."

"Isn't a Bloodmage better suited to this than Priests?" I asked. I was panting and trying not to pass out. I mean, I understood the process of childbirth at an academic level. But it never occurred to me that 'assist' meant 'deliver.'

"A Bloodmage can deliver the child, but their domain is solely the physical aspects of the birth. The Priest is the arbiter of the soul."

"We are taught that even Hessa doesn't judge the soul," I said.

"This is true, and whether or not she does is Her concern," the Master Priest said. "The Priest acts as arbiter, not as judge, but as intercessor. We guide the soul. We are the intermediaries between Hessa, the mother, and the babe. Hessa is the Goddess of Death and Life, Evan. Trust me when I say this, there is no time the veil is thinner than childbirth. Childbirth is the ultimate liminal space. This is where the Priest truly lives, and where he is most powerful."

"Oh, Hessa." I was near to hyperventilating. "But I don't know how to deliver a baby. Shouldn't I read a book first or something?"

Master Gwynn's laughter shocked me from my panic. "Not everything, you will discover, is best learned from books, my boy." He opened the door to the shrine and beckoned me inside. "You won't be doing the delivery anyway, I will. I assume you are capable of following directions?"

I scowled at him, regaining some measure of composure before we entered, and nodded. We pressed on and he smiled warmly to the expectant mother laying on the altar.

I don't know why that surprised me, but for a moment it did. The altar was as I had always seen it. It was stone, with a short ridge around the edges. There were a few chairs placed in the one-room space, and flowers sat in pots in front of the colored glass windows. Lanterns hung from hooks to further brighten the room. The incense that burned in a censor in one corner smelled strongly of soothing spices, and I sneezed twice before I could get the door shut behind us. The altar was piled with blankets and pillows, upon which the mother lay. She wore a long loose nightgown and looked to have been covered with a blanket at one point, but it was thrown aside. Her face, hair and gown dripped with sweat, and an Apprentice Bloodmage attended her, dabbing her forehead with a damp cloth.

"Mistress Helen, I hear the time is near," Master Gwynn said.

"Thank the Queen you're here, Brother," Helen said. "The healer has been helpful, but if he tells me it will be 'fine' one more time, I will throttle him with my baby's birth cord."

Master Gwynn laughed and brushed the woman's damp hair from her face. "He's only trying to help, Helen."

She reached up, grasped the young healer's hand, and squeezed it gently. "I'm sorry," she said with genuine contrition.

The Apprentice Bloodmage smiled warmly. "There's nothing to apologize for."

"You are dismissed, Uric. Thank you for your help. We will take it from here."

The Apprentice gave a slight bow and left.

"Now, Helen, this is Evan. He will be the one telling you it's fine from here on."

She smiled at me weakly. "So long as he doesn't mind getting strangl—*aagh!*" Suddenly she curled forward, and her knees rose as she let out her scream. What was she doing? Was she pushing? Hessa's tits, the baby is coming now!

"What do I do Master?" I cried.

"Hold her hands, boy."

I grabbed her hands and pinned them to the altar, restraining her.

"No, Son. Don't hold her down." He shook his head in amusement. "Just hold her hands. Comfort her, for Hessa's sake."

I relaxed my hold, and she grabbed my hands as she doubled up again. I felt my joints grind together as the woman nearly crushed them. When she collapsed at the end of her spasm, her grip weakened, and I flexed my battered fingers.

"Oh yes," Master Gwynn said. "We are close now." He laid out two pieces of thread and a thin knife on the alter near her foot, then touched her ankle which peeked from beneath her sweat soaked gown. "I'm going to take a look, Helen. Don't be alarmed." He raised her gown and arranged it about her hips. "Soon now. Good."

Master Gwynn's idea of 'soon' and my own were vastly different. It seemed as though weeks had passed before he announced that he could see the baby's head. As soon as he did, Helen's tone changed.

She let out a scream that made the hairs on my neck stand erect. She gnashed her teeth and flung her head from side to side. I looked to Master Gwynn, who stood there with his eyes narrowed and brow furrowed in worry.

"Something is wrong," he said. "The baby. The baby is taking too much."

Helen's eyes had rolled back, and her head lolled senselessly.

"What does that mean?" I asked in alarm.

"It means," the Master Priest snapped, "that we must separate the mother's soul and save the child."

"I don't understand," I said.

"We have to cut Helen's soul loose and deliver the baby. We can only save one."

I reeled. This couldn't be happening. Another child alone in the world. This couldn't be. Hessa couldn't allow such a thing. How dare she allow such a thing!

"No," I said simply.

"What?" Master Gwynn said.

"Not acceptable. We have to save them," I said.

"You don't understand," the Priest said. "I can't save them both, and the baby has nearly taken all its mother's spirit."

"We can't allow it. Do something," I demanded.

"Do what?" Gwynn screamed.

"You said the Priest is the arbiter. Intercede on their behalf, damn you."

Master Gwynn narrowed his eyes at me and sighed. "Very well. If we're going to defy a Goddess, then let's do it right. May Hessa forgive us. Come here, boy."

I pulled my fingers from Helen's weak grip and made my way to where Master Gwynn stood. He moved to Helen's head and placed his hands on her chest.

"What do I do?" I begged.

"Deliver the baby. I will contain the mother's spirit as best I can. I can't keep her from dying, but if you can separate the two souls, then perhaps it will return to her body. She is healthy, but it really depends on her will to live."

"I don't understand," I yelled.

"Usually when someone dies, it is because their body has failed, either through injury, disease, or age. She isn't dying because she is weak, she is dying because her baby is taking her soul along with its own. Normally, we would sever the mother's soul to prevent it from taking too much and they would both recover. Helen is beyond that now. I can't prevent her from dying. No one can do that. With luck, though, you can separate the child from its mother, but you must hurry."

"I don't know how to do that!" I cried as I looked between the woman's legs and saw a head protruding. "Aagh." I dove and cupped my hand under the baby's head. "Alright, now what?" I was panting, and sweat dripped into my eyes.

"Gently pull the baby free. And for Hessa's sake, don't drop it," Master Gwynn said.

I felt a pulse of power and looked to Helen. "She's barely breathing," I said.

"She is trying to go to her baby. She is not resisting the child's pull," Master Gwynn said through gritted teeth.

"The Bloodmage—" I began.

"—can't help here," Master Gwynn interrupted though gritted teeth.

Holding the baby's head, I ran my fingers in and along its body and, finding it's armpit, I gently pulled. The baby came all at once, eager to be in the world, and I stood with a child cradled in my hands.

"Place her on her mother's stomach and take up the strings I laid out, "Master Gwynn said. The struggle in his voice was plain, and I hurried to comply. He talked me through tying two strings around the cord that joined the mother and child.

"Now take the knife and cut between the bindings. Normally, we wouldn't be in a rush, but you have to separate the mother and child completely. It starts with the body."

I took the knife and firmly cut the membranous cord. When I did, Helen let out another scream. I looked in panic to see Master Gwynn, eyed closed and brows furrowed, chanting under his breath. I could feel his magic thrum throughout the room, and Helen's body convulsed. I looked at the cut and saw a thin band of shadow still connecting the baby to her mother even between the parted flesh of the cord.

"Master?" I warned.

"Separate them. I am doing all I can to keep her from Hessa's embrace."

"But I don't know how."

"Nobody does," he snapped. "We would be swaddling the babe and preparing her mother for the fire now, but you insisted on saving them both. No one has done this before. Now draw on your power and do it, or they will both die today."

I knew of only one way to draw on my power, so I did that. My body nearly trembled with the rush of strength and energy.

"Silver indeed," came a whispered gasp from Master Gwynn, but I didn't have time to pay him any mind.

The shadowy vapor of spirit flowed steadily from the mother to her child. Things I had heard of motherhood suddenly made sense. Mothers were well known for giving all for their children. I suspected that Helen knew, on some level, that it would be one or the other, and she was giving freely of herself to ensure her baby's survival. I reached out with my power and grasped her spirit. I pulled it to my silver eyes and spoke softly, "Go back." The spirit struggled to continue on to her child, but I held her firm. "Go back. She will need you more than you know."

The spirit stopped its flailing and slowly retreated. Color had just started to return to Helen's cheeks when the filmy cord stretched taught and halted.

Helen's body convulsed again, and Master Gwynn cursed and restarted his chanting, color leaving his own face from the effort.

I snatched at the cord and withdrew it in its entirety—from the mother and the child. The two shades were of slightly differing tones. The mass of souls lashed at my hand and arm as I held it in my fingers.

"You stop that," I chided. "Give it back. It's not yours." The shade stopped and twitched violently. I gave a gentle shake. "Spit it out. You need a mother more. Trust me on this." It flailed one last time, then disgorged a great plume of shadow, which retreated into her mother.

The tiny soul, so full of life and energy, spun around my hand, then wrist, all the way to my elbow and back to my fingertips. I stared at her in wonder, a stupid grin on my face. She was beautiful and I could hear her emotions, her glee at being free of the cramped prison of her mother's womb.

"What are you doing?" Master Gwynn said, his voice full of awe.

"We're playing," I said, wiggling my fingers as she sped around them. "She's beautiful. Ow!"

"What happened?" Master Gwynn asked in a panic.

"She bit me, Little Goblin."

"Evan," he said gently, the strain on his voice lessened with the return of Helen's soul. "Her body will die if she does not return to it."

I looked to Helen's stomach. It rose and fell gently. She was unconscious. But the baby's chest was still. Her lips were blue.

I knew that I needed to do something, but I didn't know what. I had separated the child and the mother, and separately, they were fine, but if this child, whose soul was so firmly wrapped about my hand did not return to her own body, she would never have a chance.

I heard it then. It was as if my earliest memories at the temple had come to life. From the first night, and for many more, when I was troubled or afraid, I would hear music. I thought it my own lullaby. As I grew, I stopped hearing it and eventually convinced myself that it was the fanciful imaginings of an orphaned child. It was real now. I felt it in my soul as it reverberated throughout the small chamber. At first I hummed along, and the young shade entwined in my fingers calmed and slowed her racing path around my arm.

I didn't recall, even in my earliest memories, ever hearing the words, but I knew them now and sang them with the full force of my voice and my magic as I guided the sleepy spirit into the breast of the little girl that lay across her mother's stomach.

With tear-filled eyes we meet at last, I've longed to see your face.
Born of love and hope and life. I yearn for your embrace.
I hold you near and kiss your cheek, your eyes in joy at last I meet.
Until in peace you find your sleep, I welcome you home.
Welcome home, Little One. Welcome home.

I turned the child over and gave her backside a smack. She took a deep breath and squalled the most beautiful sound I had ever heard. At her daughter's wail, Helen's eyes flew wide, and her arms grasped frantically for her baby. I placed the child in her arms as she unlaced her sodden nightrobe. The baby's cries ceased as she found her mother's breast and Helen shook with heavy, silent sobs.

"You'll have your hands full with this one," I whispered. "Mind her well."

Helen looked up into my silver eyes and managed a croaked, "Iela."

I smiled broadly. "A beautiful name." I released my draw and collapsed to my knees, held upright only by my hand on the altar.

Master Gwynn was silent as he studied me. After a long moment, he gathered me up and helped me to a chair. I slumped forward, my head in my hands and elbows on my knees. The room spun slowly. He left the shrine for a few minutes and returned with several strong Novices and a litter to carry mother and child to a room to rest and recover. Once they were away and we were alone, he stood over me.

"What was that?" Master Gwynn demanded.

"What do you mean?" I looked at him, and his face betrayed a mix of anger and fascination.

"You just scolded the spirit of a newborn into releasing her mother, who was all but dead."

"She was being petulant," I said. I thought it was obvious.

Master Gwynn threw up his hands in frustration. "Petulant," he muttered. "And what was that ritual you performed at the end? I am a Master Priest. I have been studying these things my entire life. I have never heard that ritual before. Hessa's tits, Evanar, I've never even heard that language!"

I flushed with anger and opened my mouth in defiance, then closed it and sagged. I didn't have the energy for anger. "That wasn't a ritual. It was a lullaby, I think. I don't know."

"That was a ritual. I could feel the power in it. It was overwhelming. I've not seen the like before." Master Gwynn sagged. "Can you walk?"

"I, um, I think so?" I said, hesitantly.

"Come then. We are getting to the bottom of you once and for all."

I rose and wobbled. "What do you mean?"

"I mean you told me that the Keeper saw something bound inside you with magic that is beyond even him. You can draw better than any Guardian, but it makes you want to hurt people. You can heal yourself, and today you perform a ritual that shouldn't be possible in a language that I've never even heard of." Master Gwynn was half panting and half grinning at the ridiculousness of having said it all at once. "We will unwrap you and figure this out."

"Is that wise?" I asked, following him to the door.

"Nothing we did today was wise," he said. "But it still worked."

"Master Brenn says that if it works, it's not dumb." I paused, then added, "He also says, 'If it's not broken, don't fix it till it is.'"

"I think Tomas is smarter than all of us."

The Beast Within

I took a deep breath and let it out. "What do you want me to do?" I asked, my voice heavy with dread. We were back in the classroom. Master Gwynn had Ellyn light the brazier, then dismissed her for the day, telling her to inform the others that class was postponed and we were not to be disturbed.

"I want you to draw, and I will observe you."

My hands began to sweat. "I don't want to hurt you, I said, "Or worse,"

Master Gwynn nodded. "You didn't hurt Helen or her child. Quite the opposite, in fact. I know you get aggressive the more you draw on your power, but I believe you can control it better than you think. I assure you, I wouldn't attempt this if I weren't confident."

I nodded and reluctantly drew upon my spirit.

The instant I did, I felt my anxiety fade, replaced with the rush of strength and energy that I normally associated with drawing. I could feel the emotions roil inside me, the hunger and the need to lash out, and I reigned in the power.

"No," the Master said. "Draw deeper. Pull more." I hesitated, but did as he commanded. I pulled ever deeper on that well of power that was my soul. All of my emotions intensified as the room dimmed. I focused, and the shadows on the walls replayed the birth from this morning. Power flew about the room in shadowed parody. The illumination of the lanterns and the brazier faded until there was a kind of balance. The room settled to a gray haze that just seemed natural. Everything seemed to spin. Was I on the verge of losing consciousness? I clenched my hands into fists and leaned forward to get a scent of the man across from me. He smelled… delicious. The upswell of aggression and the promise of violence bubbled up in my throat and I heard myself chuckle.

"More," Master Gwynn said eagerly. I squeezed my fists and felt the skin under my fingertips part as I resisted the burning need to hurt the Priest, this thing that had caught my attention. This… prey? Was it prey? I pulled ever more. My breath came in labored gasps, and my heart pounded in my chest. It was not exertion but anticipation. Anticipation of what, I couldn't say.

My eyes were closed, and I tried to huddle in on myself to keep from hurting this creature. Why must we protect it? My nostrils flared, and I caught a new scent rolling off him in waves. Fear.

So, it is prey, I thought, silently hoping it would run.

I heard a gasp of surprise and opened my eyes to see it scrambling backwards away from us, hands and feet clawing at the ground. I exploded to my feet amidst the flickering shadows. The shadows moved unnaturally, yet the motion was familiar and comforting.

It opened its mouth and spoke, but I couldn't hear the words. All I could hear was the roar in my ears. I concentrated on its face and crouched on all fours. Its eyes widened further as its back struck the wall and could retreat no more.

After a moment, I heard it.

"Evanar?" it said. "Evanar. Are you in there?"

I could barely hear the sound over the rushing in my ears. Then I realized it was just my laughter. It was a satisfied sound and mocking. It mocked its attempt at escape.

"Evan, if you're in there, you need to assert your will, boy," it said gaining some backbone and rising from his crouch along the wall.

I heard him. As I pushed back against the laughter and the hunger that poured from my chest, I felt more myself.

"Master Gwynn," I said, but the sound that came forth was a mockery of my voice. It was strange and harmonic, as though there were two or more speaking from within my throat. All the voices were higher or lower than my own, but they were my voice.

Master Gwynn straightened his robe and stared at me in awe. "Blessed Queen," he whispered the familiar prayer. "In the end we find beginning. In the beginning, we find home. Born of you and received by you. What madness have you brought into this world that I might despair?"

I flinched at his desecration of the scripture. He took a step forward. "Stay back," I hissed. "I don't want to hurt you."

"You didn't hurt the child or the mother."

I felt a resurgence of the power within me, and I felt my control slipping. "I do not hunt the weak. I defend it. They are mine."

"Evanar!" he barked. "Assert your will."

His forcefulness shocked me, and I regained a semblance of control.

"No. I don't believe you will harm me," he said and advanced slowly.

"And if I do?" I asked.

"Then we'll both learn something, will we not?"

He reached out, hesitantly took my hand, and held it up for me to see. I didn't know what I was looking at. What I saw was not a hand but a claw. Three long silver talons tipped slender fingers, much like a raptor. Looking down at my chest, I realized I was naked, my clothes lay in a tattered heap at my feet. I ran my tongue over needle-sharp teeth, and my fingers probed at smooth black skin that covered my body. The joints on my legs were reversed, like a dog or a bird, but heavily muscled and tipped in sharp silver talons—much like my hands but larger. Noticeably larger.

"What has happened to me?" I gasped. Fear rose in my chest. "What did you do to me?" I grabbed the Priest by his shoulders, easily lifting his feet from the ground. He winced in pain, and I immediately regretted my action and set him down. "I'm sorry, Master. I didn't mean —"

"It's okay, my boy, you're very strong," he mused. "Stronger than I would have given you credit. To answer your question, though, I did nothing to you. It's you."

"I didn't do this," I said, tapping myself on the chest with one razor sharp talon.

"I didn't say you did it," the Priest said, "I said it's you. This—" he gestured at my bestial appearance— "this form is you, just as much as the Evanar you see in the mirror every morning… just another aspect."

Just. Another. Aspect.

"Well, make it go away," I cried. "Bring me back."

"I can't, Evan. You have to." He reached out and placed his hand flat against my chest. He closed his eyes and concentrated. I felt warmth spread over me, then in an instant it was gone as I snarled and smacked the Priest's hand away.

He looked at me, eyes wide in surprise and, I noticed, not a little fear. "It's your magic," he said. "Your power is not like the Guardians. It is so much more. You can draw like a Guardian, but that power weakens the bonds that hold this aspect of you in check."

"Aspect," I hissed. "You keep calling me an Aspect, calling this an Aspect."

"I don't know what else to call it. It is clearly you. You are clearly it. Yet, you are so different, and so similar." He chuffed. "Then again, the more I learn of you, the more familiar and different you seem. Yet another Aspect."

"You talk in circles," I spat. "I can draw. I am a Guardian."

"You can use your soul to increase your speed and strength, yes," he said. "Your power is also similar to the Priests, but you can do what I cannot, Evan. I could have saved the child by killing her mother, because I could not touch their spirits. You pulled them free like twine from a top and toyed with them. No, my boy. Your soul is your magic. It binds this Aspect of you inside you. The more you use it, the more of this Aspect of you leaks through."

"The Keeper said something similar when I compared myself to a Bleeder."

Master Gwynn slashed at the air with his hand in anger. "Never use that term again!" he snarled. His face was red and, forgetting his fear, he took a step forward and poked my muscled, black-skinned chest for emphasis. "It is an archaic word for something humanity is too ignorant to understand. I will not have a student of mine use it. Ever! Am I understood?"

Of a sudden, the scene struck me as amusing. Here was this middle-aged Priest, berating a monster for using a slur. I laughed. The sound was unnerving, even in my ears. Master Gwynn realized this at the same time and withdrew his finger, looking a bit chagrined. He cleared his throat.

"I believe that your training with the Guardians, your constant drawing, has weakened the bonds that conceal and bind this Aspect of you. By drawing so much since the assessment, you have weakened these bonds even further, and your Aspect has fully manifested. I don't know why this was bound or hidden, but it is out now."

"Get rid of it," I begged.

Master Gwynn's face softened. "I would have to kill you to be rid of it Evanar. You are not understanding. It is you, and now it is loose. We will have to learn to subdue it again. You will never be rid of it, nor should you want to be."

"Look at me!" I roared. "Why would I not want to be rid of this?"

"Because nothing has changed, Evan," Gwynn said.

"Everything has changed. Just look at me."

"I see you. I hear you. I hear, albeit oddly, Evanar Hostric panicking because something is different from what he perceived a moment ago."

"Different," I chuffed. "Monstrous more like it."

"Like the monster that ate the child this morning?"

"I didn't eat that child! I saved her!"

Master Gwynn gave me a knowing grin directed at my thoughtless, self-imposed hatred. It was a hatred without basis. Uncles Tamil and Zai, and the rest of my Templar family, taught me better than to hate blindly. Master Gwynn showed me that the lesson also applied to myself.

"So how do I get me back?" I asked. "I still feel the hunger, and I still crave the violence. Can I get back to me? To what I am used to?"

"You have to assert your will over the Aspect of yourself that you wish to control, then ground yourself, holding true to the image of who you know yourself to be."

"I don't know how to do that," I said.

"Then pay attention."

I calmed myself as best I could with the boiling emotions of my Aspect, mixed with my fear, churning inside me.

"Identify something you can see," the Master said. His voice was soothing and calm and jarred the tide of feelings that I struggled to contain.

"I can see you."

"Don't describe it to me. This isn't a test. Focus on what you can see." He gave me a moment to arrest my attention. "Now, something you can smell."

With a clear image of the man firmly in my mind, I closed my eyes and breathed deep. The strongest smell in the room was the head of smoke from the brazier as it drifted up and through a hole in the ceiling. I breathed in the scent that was so common in the worship spaces throughout the temple, this Temple I called home. I felt myself calm.

"Something you can hear."

I strained my attention, eyes still closed and breathing in the fire's scent, and could hear the faint sizzle of the coals as the flame crackled and popped. I nearly had to hold my breath to hear it, the sound was so slight.

"Something you can taste."

I thought for a moment, then had an idea. I opened my hand and observed the small puncture wounds in my palms and the smear of blood that was even now drying on my skin. I licked it. The copper, metallic taste filled my senses, and I calmed even further.

"Now, something you are. Know your sense of self, who you are, what you are. Know that. Know it will all your being."

I wobbled unsteadily on my bare feet and nearly tripped over the mound of shredded clothes below me. I gawked at my hands. They were normal. I laughed. It was a silly sound, a plain monotone in my own ears. Master Gwynn caught me before I hit the floor and laid me gently beside the brazier to keep me warm. I felt him leave my side and heard a door open and close. He wrapped a warm blanket around my naked body. Even with the fire near, I was cold.

"It's all right, my boy," he said in a calm, gentle tone. "You did well. We will get through this together. I will help you."

Feeding

I worked with Master Gwynn a great deal over the next few weeks. At first, it took away from my time training with the Guardians. We both figured that was for the best, as extended training sessions with the Guardians left me agitated and hostile. With a considerable amount of practice, I was finally able to control the change from my normal self to my Aspect, and back, at will. There were some limitations, but I was getting better.

When I did return to the training ground, it was raining. We had been just standing there for some time. I was certain that not only was my armor waterlogged, but my skin was as well. Fog hung thick around us, and with the torrents of water falling into our eyes, we could barely see.

"The enemy won't write to you asking if the weather is to your liking for a grand battle. No, they will just stick a blade in your gut. A good rainstorm is the perfect time for an ambush, especially if you're weak," Master Brenn said. "Your pitiful body is cold and wet. Your armor chafes. You are shivering and wondering if the wetness under your nose is the rain or illness." He continued his lecture as we stood there like drowned rats, miserable and wishing for a warm fire and some of Master Gregor's stew.

"But you must be vigilant," he continued. "Complacency carries a keener edge than any weapon. Your enemies are all about you. They plot your demise. They search for the optimum time to strike, when you are focused inward, rather than looking outward for threats that lurk within the liquid sunshine."

With those last two words, even over the sound of the rain, which muffled everything, I heard swords beings drawn.

My feet flew from under me, and I hit the ground with a *whuff*. The breath left my body. My eyes widened in shock as I saw Mallus bearing down on me with his sword, eyes gray and face intent.

I rolled to my feet, then slipped in the wet mud and fell again. I struggled to get my legs under me, but Mallus wasn't giving me the chance. If he had, I would have thought less of him. He was taught better than that. I scrambled backward and, realizing that I could not get away in that manner, changed tactics.

I drew, my eyes immediately flashing to silver, and I kicked out with both feet. He was ready for the move and stutter-stepped to halt his momentum for just a moment and keep from being kicked. A moment was all I needed. With my enhanced speed, I rolled back and to my feet and drew my sword in the same motion. I barely got my blade in front of Mallus's as he pressed his advantage.

Already on the defensive, I retreated to create distance and assess my surroundings. It was difficult with Mallus trying to take my head off at every opportunity. From what I could tell, the class was broken in half and those chosen to be the aggressors in Brenn's machinations had attacked those nearest them. Everyone had broken into their pairs and were spread out, fighting desperately while Master Brenn stood in the middle of the chaos, laughing at the mayhem he had created. He had set this up to prove a point. It was well made, considering the situation on the field.

I thought I saw Alanis through the fog and rain, on his back and blocking furiously as someone pounded him from a standing position. Meri was already down. I couldn't see her, as I had retreated even further from the group, but I heard a familiar stream of curses that drifted through the fog.

As Mallus pressed my retreat, I looked for an opening. There wasn't one. We traded blow after blow, distancing ourselves ever further from the rest of the trainees. Mallus had always been a talented fighter, and with the added training of the more advanced techniques, his performance at that point left no doubt that he would be a Master one day. I tried several times to get through his barrage of strikes and cuts. Every attempt failed.

I jumped back to avoid a nasty cut and was too slow. The edge of his blunted blade caught my side, and I felt a rib crack through my armor. Instantly enraged, I abandoned all technique and charged him. I hit him hard and rode him to the ground. Both his blade and mine were lost in the mist and fog, and I found myself sitting atop my friend, fully Aspected, with silver talons wrapped around his neck. He was unconscious.

A squeeze. A twist. All over for our valiant adversary.

No. This is training, I thought as I asserted my will and subdued my monstrous Aspect. Just then I heard my name being called through the fog. I wrapped the beast in tendrils of magic as I had been practicing. I was getting better at this. I had lost myself for a moment, but I could wrest it back under control. I was improving.

A voice called out for me again.

"Here, Ivey," I yelled. I scrambled to redress before she found me, my clothes and armor having passed through my shadowy form as I transitioned. She came into view just as I was slipping my sodden cuirass of crossed leather back over my head.

"What is taking you so long?" she asked, noting Mallus unconscious at my feet. "Oh. We thought sure he had you. If anyone could get you, it was him. Anyway, the exercise is over and Master Brenn wants to debrief. And why was your armor off?"

I nodded toward Mallus. "I think he cracked one of my ribs. Help me look for our swords. I'll carry Mallus back. Master Brenn will want to get him checked out."

After the debrief, followed by a change of dry clothes and a hot meal, I was relaxing in my room and studying when the thought occurred to me that I did not feel that lingering sense of anger after training. I'd expected it, and its absence was jarring. Perhaps I was getting stronger.

I noticed the shadows on my wall. The lantern's flame reacted wildly in the breeze from my open shutters, but the shadows made lazy swirls, as though they couldn't be bothered to react. I set my book aside and reached out. I touched the wall and watched the shadows spin lethargically around my fingers where they touched. I removed my hand, and they returned to their slowly shifting pattern. I reached out one finger and touched the wall, not trying to touch the shadows. They continued their meandering dance.

I wondered if they had fled previously because I expected them to. They seemed to have been playing out my thoughts, and when I noticed them, they retreated, unwilling to be discovered. I had grown in my power since then, and I wasn't afraid of it anymore. With the assumption that the shadows would react to my will, like little Iela had, I placed my fingers back to the wall and called to them. They flocked to my hand and coalesced into something almost solid. I pulled my hand away, and they dispersed back along the wall, content in their wanderings.

I touched the wall a third time and willed them to come to me. They did so in a rush. I pulled my hand away, maintaining my call, and they streamed from the wall in a translucent gray line and pooled in my palms. I sat there on my bed, my hands cupped, holding a writhing ball of living shadow. It spun and slithered, and I could feel it against my skin. I grinned like a boy with a new toy.

For a fortnight, before bed, I practiced and learned all that I could regarding the shadows and my Aspect. Master Gwynn helped me. He poked and prodded and tested, and we tried everything we could think of to learn about my Aspect and my power. I could bring forth my Aspect now at will, but the process was taxing. I learned many new tricks. There were things still, however, that neither of us understood.

"It's time to show the Keeper," Master Gwynn said.

"Are you sure?" I asked. "Do you think I am strong enough, have enough control?

"You are. You do." Master Gwynn nodded. "I have done all I can. We have learned much, but there is still much that is beyond me. The Keeper may know more. Besides, you have been itching to do this from the moment you Aspected the first time."

I gave him a mischievous grin. "Tamil is here, too. I saw him arrive this morning."

Gwynn narrowed his eyes. "What are you planning?"

I didn't answer. I turned and headed for the door. I stopped with my hand on the latch and turned back to Master Gwynn. He had helped me so much. Without him, I would never have made it this far. I shuddered to think what would have happened without his guidance and willingness to help me. I smiled at the elder Priest. "Thank you, Uncle."

He returned my smile and gave a nod. I shut the door behind me.

I made my way to the Keeper's office.

"Hello Inec, is the Keeper in?" I asked the Priest. The man nodded and waved me toward the door.

"The Magister is in there with him, but he didn't tell me they were not to be disturbed."

I nodded my thanks and knocked. A voice from the other side bade me enter, and I did, closing the door behind me.

The Keeper sat at his desk and Tamil sat across from him. A bottle of wine was open between them. They were laughing at something as I entered.

"Evan, it's good to see you," Tamil said as he rose and hugged me, then retook his seat.

"You too, Uncle. I am glad you're here. There's something I want to show you both."

"This sounds ominous," the Keeper said, refilling his cup. "Gwynn said there was a situation during a birth and you helped to save the mother and babe. Congratulations."

"Thank you," I said, taking the other chair, "but that was just the beginning of several discoveries."

"What did you learn?" Tamil said with a grin as he delivered his favorite teaching tool. I grinned back at him.

"Remember my assessment, when I drew for the first time?" Both men nodded. "Everyone said they thought they saw shadows, but since none understood it, it was mostly forgotten." They nodded again.

I leaned over and called to my shadow, that lay just under my chair, and it sped to my hand. I held out the swirling mass in front of me. It twisted and played over my palm, then lengthened and began wrapping itself around hand and wrist and arm, much like the spirit of the child did. I smiled at it.

"Fascinating," Uncle Zai said, leaning forward in his chair. His eyes were unfocused, and I could tell he was using his ability to see into the power I was using. "How?"

"I don't know, Uncle, I just know that I can."

"What do you see?" Tamil asked.

The Keeper's gaze righted itself, and he looked at me in astonishment. "Those aren't shadows. They are souls."

"Like what you do?" Tamil asked.

"Not exactly. What I do is with my soul," Zai said. "These souls, and yes there are several, are not Evan's own, yet they are. They *belong* to him."

Their eyes met then, and it was as though something passed between them, some kind of communication that I wasn't privy to.

"There's more," I said. "Uncle Zai. You mentioned your own power. Would you mind?" I dismissed my shadows and gestured for him to use his own.

He looked at me with suspicion, but complied. A thin, dark, whip-like tendril snaked from his palm and drifted toward me. I reached out my hand and flicked it with my finger. The Keeper flinched at the sudden contact and threw himself backward into his chair. He gasped in shock, and his power retreated within him in a flash.

Tamil burst out in laughter.

"How did you do that?" Uncle Zai asked. His face held disbelief and amazement. "That's impossible. Even the Priests cannot touch another's soul. They act upon it, but can't interact with it."

"Oh, that's great!" Tamil said in between fits of laughter. He wiped tears from his eyes. "You should see the look on your face. It's priceless."

"I'm glad you think so, Uncle," I said, then gave a wink to the Keeper and dropped into the shadows.

That was what it felt like. It was as though I moved my body and became one with the spirits that were a part of me. I fell, incorporeal, and the shadows splashed over my chair, leaving my clothing where they landed. I drifted along the floor in a thin haze.

"What the… What did you do? Where are you, boy?" Tamil cried.

I appeared behind him, fully Aspected. "Here, Uncle."

The Keeper made a choking noise, but the Magister of the Realm and First Consult to the Emperor squeaked like a startled girl as he toppled over in his chair. He lay on his back, eyes wide in shock and fear at what he saw before him. In his defense, he did have a dagger in his hand by the time he hit the floor.

I extended a hand to Tamil, an offer to help him rise. He looked at the silver talons and hesitantly reached out and grasped one sharp claw. I pulled him to his feet. As soon as he was up, he stepped back, wary.

"Evan?" he croaked.

"It's me, Uncle," I said in that odd harmonic voice.

He slid the dagger back up his sleeve.

I cocked my head at him. "Neat trick."

Uncle Tamil looked all about him then, as though searching for something.

"Occupational necessity," He mumbled. "How are you doing that?"

"Doing what?" I replied.

"It sounds like you are talking from everywhere at once. Hessa's tits, boy, but that's creepy."

"Tamil!" the Keeper scolded.

"Come on, Zai, you've seen the statues."

Zaipheth Ren straightened indignantly. "Hessa's bare breast represents her life giv—"

"I know what it represents, you officious bastard. But you can only cry, 'Great Queen,'" Tamil flailed his hands about as though in panic, "so much before you have to make fun of even yourself."

At this point, I was laughing so hard I nearly toppled while putting on my trousers. Both men looked at me, startled, their argument all but forgotten.

"How long have you two been arguing over this?" I asked.

"Years," said Uncle Zai.

Tamil started to say something, but a glare from the Keeper changed his mind.

"Longer than we care to admit," he said instead.

I shook my head.

Zai rose and came around his desk. He gestured toward me. "May I?" He wanted to read me. I nodded. He touched my chest, and I felt his cool power seep slowly into my skin. I suppressed my Aspect's natural tendency to retaliate against the intrusion.

"What do you see, Zai?" Tamil asked.

"He's in there. He is still bound, but the bonds seem... flexible, Zaipheth Ren said.

"As in it can get loose?" Tamil asked.

"As in I can let it loose, if I choose," I said. "I have been doing that in some small measure since the assessment, it seems. It is the nature of my power. From what Master Gwynn and I have been able to discern, I draw by siphoning away some of the magic that the binding uses to restrain this Aspect of me. The more I use, the more can seep through. That is where the aggression comes from. Now that I know about it, I can regulate it."

"What happens if it breaks free completely?" Tamil asked.

"We don't think it can, completely," I said. "I don't know what event could cause that, but Master Gwynn believes that eventually it would be subdued by the spells that bound it in the first place. He also thinks it would take something extreme to bring it on. As it stands, I can control it."

"As is stands?" the Keeper asked.

"Well, some days are better than others. The more I use my power, the more difficult it is to control the aggression and the urges. If I don't use my power, it never becomes an issue. The more I use it, however, the better I get at using it, and the more I can use before I feel the effects." I shrugged.

"It seems you have been working awfully hard," Zai said. "Keep doing what you are doing, Evan. I think you are on the right path, and I applaud you."

Uncle Tamil nodded his own approval. I had told them all I knew. They were still discussing it when I left to grab some dinner before getting back to my studies.

My routine had largely returned to normal and I was en route to meet with Ivey for sparring. She and I had become close since the day she arrived at the temple. She was so much more than my first love; she was my best friend. I smiled at that thought, as I did with any thought of her. We were to train that evening with the latest batch of techniques that Master Brenn had shown us. To get to the training grounds, I had to pass by the stables, and it so happened that Ivey was working in the stables as part of her duties. That was my destination.

As I approached, I heard a commotion inside. A muffled cry. I increased my pace, and the closer I got, the more I could hear. A thump, a groan, a whimper.

I ran. I entered the stables and slid to a halt, looking frantically for the origin of my distress. I saw flickering movement in the shadows from a stall in the back corner. I sped the length of the barn until I could determine the source. Gorse had Ivey down on her back in the hay. Her face was bloody and swollen.

He crouched over her. One hand covered her mouth as the other tore at her clothing. I felt her try to draw. Shaggy must have seen her face grow slack or the film of gray smoke cloud her eyes, because he punched her, hard, in the stomach, and I heard her try to cry out as her draw shattered.

He untied his trousers. I heard laughter bubble up from my throat as I dropped into the shadows.

I felt my clothes drift through me as they fell to the ground and I flowed as fast as thought toward my prey. I landed on his back. And sinking my talons into him, I spun and threw him into the wall of the opposite stall. The hardwood that made up the barn wall splintered and cracked. He made no sound as he fell from the broken boards to his face in the manure strewn stable.

I stepped over Ivey in my fully Aspected form, and she retreated into the straw. I flung my hands out to either side, and the shadows came to me, heeding my summons, eager to serve. I formed them with a thought and sent them at my prey. It screamed as the shadows gathered it up and slammed it back into the broken boards. Sharp tendrils of shadow pierced its flesh and buried deep into the wood beyond. It hung from shadowy spikes, a pitiful reflection of humanity.

"I gave you every opportunity to ignore me, Gorse," I said, my harmonic voice discordant in the confines of the barn. "I tried to ignore you when you were not hurting others. I even gave you a principled reason not to bother with me further. She said I should have killed you then." I jerked my head toward Ivey who pulled at her clothes to cover herself. "She was right."

I stalked toward him, teeth and talons glimmering in the faint evening light that filtered through the open doors at either end of the stables. "You refuse. That's fine. You may harangue me all you wish, *Shaggy,*" I said. He flinched as I slammed a hand on either side of his head and leaned in, two rows of razor sharp silver teeth mere inches from his face. He tried to turn his head away and whimpered. "But harm one I love? Unacceptable."

He soiled himself. The stench made even greater due to the fact that he had gotten his trousers untied before I attacked him. They hung at his knees, now soiled with his offal. He cried a piteous wail. I had no pity in me. Not for this one.

"Pathetic," I said in a derisive sneer.

I showed him a silver talon, then plunged it into his groin, his intended weapon of humiliation. I dragged the claw upward through muscle, organ, and bone until I reached his chest and withdrew it. I licked the blood from the back of my hand, my long, black tongue smeared red.

I tilted my head and studied him as one might study a bug pinned inside a picture frame. I watched, fascinated, as the light faded from his eyes and his spirit left his body. I reached out with my magic and grasped his soul out of sheer instinct and drew it into myself.

Shaggy's eyes went blank in death, but mine exploded in black fire.

I felt his soul flow into mine. His energy, his spirit, everything he intended, everything he wanted, every hate, every love, hit my soul like a searing brand. My back arched as I was lifted from the ground by the very shadows that I had used to impale Gorse Larkin to the stable wall. I looked in panic as the shadows took me. They held me aloft and twined about me in cords like thorny vines. They wrapped about my legs and arms, wrists and ankles and dug deep, burrowing into my flesh and anchoring to my soul. The pain was excruciating and exquisite. When the last of the thorns dug into my scalp, I screamed. At the end of that breath, I drew another and screamed again, this time accompanied by what sounded like dozens of beasts surrounding the temple. Every predator on the island bellowed out in triumph as power flooded over me, and in one massive convulsion, I collapsed.

The shadows faded with my Aspect, and Gorse Larkin fell to the stable floor even as I collapsed, naked and senseless. I saw Ivey staring at me in fear and wonder. I reached for her. I tried to call her name before the darkness took me.

I WOKE TO FIND TAMIL HARAN, AND IVEY, IN MY ROOM.

"How do you feel, Evan?" Tamil asked.

I couldn't remember how I got here. I scoured my memory for some clue as to what led me to be in bed at what appeared to be the middle of the day. It all came in a rush.

I lurched forward, my eyes wide and panicked. "I killed him," I said.

Uncle Tamil placed a hand on my chest and gently pushed me back into the pillows. "Yes, you did."

"I'm a murderer," I said. It was a logical conclusion, but I didn't have any emotion to express for the concept. I knew I should feel something, but I didn't. That disturbed me greatly.

"No, you're not," he said matter-of-factly. "He was a monster. You put him down, and he deserved it. The world is a better place without him in it." He said.

I felt my stomach lurch and whipped the blankets off as I rolled out of bed. Tamil moved quickly to place a pail before me as I lost the contents of my stomach.

"It's a common reaction," he said, rubbing my back as he knelt beside me on the floor. I heaved again and again. When nothing remained and my strength was spent, he helped me back into bed, and Ivey brought me a cup of cool water and some powdered soda to clean my mouth.

"You need more rest." He turned and walked past Ivey, who stood holding a steaming bowl of water between her hands, a washing cloth draped over one arm. She stood as though waiting for a cue to proceed. Uncle Tamil stood behind her, one hand on the door latch. "We'll talk later," he said. "For now, you are sick and need tended to. This young lady has hardly left your side for three days. It would be rude to not allow her to carry out her duties."

"Three days?" I rose out of surprise, but in my weakness, I moved very little for the effort.

"You're sick. You. Need. Tended. To." He gave me a look like my friends would give when we were young and being questioned by the Masters. It screamed, 'Don't screw this up.' Ivey's face flushed pink with his words.

"You have a dedicated caretaker." He glanced at Ivey, who could not see him, and then back to me. "I think you'll be in excellent hands. I'll stop by later. I need to see Zaipheth." He reached around Ivey and dropped something into the bowl. She looked into it and blushed. Tamil left without another word.

Ivey set the steaming bowl of water on the table beside my bed and eased down on the edge, careful not to jostle me. The freckles that dusted her nose and cheeks faded back to their normal hue.

"Ivey, I…" I began.

"Why didn't you tell me?" she asked in a small voice as she wrung hot water from the washing cloth. I searched her face, but she didn't meet my eyes. I had already been washed free of Gorse's blood. She bathed me anyway, focusing only on the task and the spot she was cleaning. She started with my face, gently wiping at my forehead, and then dragged the coarse cloth carefully down each cheek to my chin.

"I was afraid," I said. "I was afraid that you would reject me. I was afraid I would lose you if you knew what I had become."

She nodded slowly. "I was frightened at first. Then I heard your voice come from that... thing, and I knew it was you. She chuckled. "I could never be afraid of you." I smiled with her.

She looked at me then and smacked my bare chest. "You're an idiot. You should have told me!"

I looked down in shame. "I know."

We were both quiet for a long time. It was Ivey who broke the silence. "I'm glad you killed him. If I didn't know that he was dead already, I would go kill him now." Her eyes unfocused as she relived that moment. It was as though she was still lying in the straw, face bruised and clothes torn and hanging off of her. She looked so vulnerable. I knew that had to be the worst part for her. Ivey was many things, but vulnerable, she was not.

I felt for her then. It was not pity. Rather, I was angry on her behalf. I knew Ivey better than I knew myself, my own doubts notwithstanding. I tried to read her face, to discern her feelings on the events that had transpired there in the stables.

"What happened after you killed Gorse? That scared me," she said. "I thought you were dying."

"I'm not sure. There was something to it, though. It almost felt like a finality, like something was settled." I shook my head. "I don't know."

"When you collapsed, I tried to wake you. You wouldn't respond. The Keeper has been in here every day to check on you and mutter prayers on your behalf. He was worried, too."

"I am sorry you saw me kill Shaggy," I said. "But I'm not sorry he's dead."

"Don't you dare," She growled. Her rust-green eyes turned to flint as they bored into me. "Not after what he did, and was planning to do."

I opened my mouth to speak, but she held up a hand, halting me.

"He planned it for weeks." Anger suffused her voice. "He told me. He gloated about it while he was beating me to keep me from drawing." Her anger seeped from her skin. I could smell it. Anger...

and shame. I knew that she had suffered, but I hadn't realized how much.

"He and his friends came up with a plan to hurt you. He said every Guardian has their weakness. Mine was that I couldn't draw consistently. He knew that if I couldn't focus, then I couldn't defend myself. Your weakness, he said, is me."

She shivered at the memory. Her emotions were raw on her face as she told me. I considered telling her that she didn't have to tell me, that she didn't have to relive that, but it seemed that she needed to, on some level.

"He came up with a plan to catch me alone. He had heard that I was weak in drawing, but if I managed it, he wouldn't have a chance. So he ambushed me there in the stables, and every time I tried to draw, he beat me until I lost focus."

I didn't know what to say. I had no idea how to comfort her, as anything I could have managed would be patronizing and trite. So, I said nothing.

"When you arrived, I was relieved and ashamed," she said. "I was proud to have a powerful protector and ashamed that I needed one. Me." She scoffed. "Apprentice to some of the greatest fighters in the land, grateful for rescue."

I laid my hand over hers and gave her what I hoped was a reassuring smile.

"It was then I realized the seriousness of what we are training to do," she said. "Until now, I have been treating it as a fun adventure." She shook her head. "I know better now. I will never be so weak again."

"I'm weak as a kitten right now," I said, trying to lighten the mood.

Ivey shook herself, and her expression turned playful in the span of the motion.

"Good. That means you won't be able to defend yourself."

My brows rose, and I tried to tense for some attack, but I was too tired for any real reaction.

She fished into the washbasin and came up with a key. She crossed the room and used it on the door, securing it from entry.

She turned toward me and tugged at the lacing along the front of her tunic, revealing taut muscles and pale skin so often covered with armor as to never see the sun.

"Ivey," I started.

The washing cloth, now chilled, hit my face, and I sputtered.

"Shut up before you ruin it. I thought I had lost you, you moron," she said. "I am happy you're not dead." Her smile turned coy then. "I'm going to show you how much."

I couldn't take my eyes off her as she undressed.

"You will sleep well tonight."

Resolve

"I'm leaving the Guardians," I said.

I delivered the news as soon as everyone was seated. The Keeper sat behind his desk, and Tamil Haran took one of the two other chairs in the room. Neither of these men who raised me, men who I called Uncle, knew what this meeting was about. I had just asked to speak to both of them privately, as I figured the news I had to deliver would be unpopular. Unpopular or not, I had made my decision.

"Why?" Zaipheth Ren asked. "Because you lost control and killed someone?"

"No," I said. "Because I didn't lose control. If I had, perhaps I could learn more, do better next time. No. I decided that he needed to die. I felt nothing when I killed him, and I would do it again." Both men cocked their heads at that.

"Then you are ahead of the game," Tamil said.

The Keeper shot a scowl at his Guardian.

"Don't," Tamil said to him. "You know as well as I do that monsters are real. We have seen them firsthand." He made a nod toward the tapestry on the wall behind me of the first Guardian and Finder, locked in battle with undead at the inception of the Order of Hessa. He turned to me. "People use words like good and evil because it makes them feel superior, as if they know what side they are on. But the world is much more gray than that. So, tell me, Evan," Tamil leaned forward in challenge, "what did you learn?"

"That I don't know where I stand on that scale," I said truthfully.

"What do you mean?" Uncle Zai asked.

"I mean, I don't feel bad about it," I said. "At first, I thought it was shock, but it isn't. I just don't regret it, and I think I should."

"Look, Son. The first time you take a life is not an insignificant event, Tamil said. "In fact, believe it or not, it's quite rare. There are millions in this world who have never killed another person." He shrugged and continued, "Maybe a farmer kills an intruder bent on doing him and his family harm, but compared to all the times it doesn't happen, its negligible. Sure, there are thieves who would kill you for a loaf of bread. There are loads of stories about assassins and murderers, some that commit heinous acts but have hearts of gold." He paused. "I once read a story about an assassin with a dagger that fed off the very souls of its victims and constantly drove him to kill." He laughed.

I stiffened. *That hits close to home,* I thought.

"It's all rubbish," he continued. "A good story is just that—a good story. In real life, people outside of the legions during wartime, the vast majority of people, in fact, don't go around killing one another. The city watch doesn't even keep peace with the sword, but with the sap."

"I believe, Uncle, that I have more in common with your assassin-wielding dagger than the city guardsman."

"What do you mean?" Tamil asked.

"I didn't just kill Gorse, Uncle." I reached out and pulled a handful of shadows from about the room, including my own. They danced in my palm, eager to play, or serve, whatever I desired. "I ate his soul." I could not believe that I would have ever said these words before now. I didn't know such a thing was possible, but I was certain about what had happened. I remember my feelings at the time of his death and the explosion of power and pain that had accompanied it.

"Ate?" the Keeper asked.

"I took his soul into me. I made it part of me. Don't ask me how I know this, but he is in here, somewhere." I released the shadows and they dispersed in into gray wisps.

"So?" Tamil asked.

"So, it's not right. I know that the Priests help the souls of the dying to return to Hessa and thus feed the Queen and her power for the Order. I didn't feed the Queen. I fed myself."

The Keeper and his Guardian looked at each other. Tamil's face was smug, while Uncle Zai's was sour.

"So what is the problem?" Tamil asked.

"The problem is, I ate him!" I exclaimed.

Tamil reached over to the Keeper's desk and withdrew a blank sheet of parchment. "Use your shadows," he said and tossed the paper into the air. I made a slashing motion with my hand, and shadows trailed after my fingers. From three feet away, the paper parted and fell in two pieces to the floor.

"In my mind, you have finally made him useful," said Tamil.

"It's not right. Doesn't he deserve to go back to Hessa? I have denied him that."

"What do you want?" Uncle Zai asked. "You want us to tell you that you did the right thing? That you did the wrong thing? It doesn't work like that. Honestly, if I had caught Gorse Larkin instead of you, he would be just as dead. A thin, black, flame-like tendril rose from the Keeper's palm. "It would have just been a bit less messy." The sliver of his soul retreated beneath his skin. "Does that help you?"

"Not really." I fell into the empty chair.

"So what are you going to do?"

I sat there for a time thinking over what they said. "I will stay with the Priesthood. I won't have to kill, nor be concerned that I am going to eat someone. I can still serve the Order."

"That's fine," the Keeper said. "Your path is your own. We only wanted you to grow into the best man you could be. That you are so thoughtful and concerned now tells me you will do fine in whatever you choose. I believe, however, that you have a role to fill in the world and within the Order that none of us have yet to realize."

I hugged them both before I left. I was grateful to them, and grateful for them. They had always been there for me, and I found myself awed at the support they provided. It was with these thoughts and a smile on my face that I entered the sanctuary to begin a fresh life in the Priesthood of Hessa.

"Hi Ellyn," I said as I entered the ritual space, much lighter in spirit than I thought I would. "Are you taking extra shifts? You're here nearly every time I come in."

"No, you're just lucky, I guess," Ellyn replied, her smile bright as ever and her finger twirling her curly, blonde hair as was her habit. "So how did it go with the Keeper?"

"Better than expected, actually," I said. "Wait. How did you know?"

Ellyn giggled. "Master Gwynn mentioned that you would be around the class more from now on, so I guessed. It suits me fine to spend more time with you," she said, her smile growing ever wider.

"You know that nothing else has changed, right? Ivey and I are still firmly together."

"I know," she said. "Everyone knows. I am patient, though."

I narrowed my eyes at her. "What do you mean you're 'patient?'"

"It's obvious," she said, the smile slowly fading from her face and replaced with concern. "Isn't it?" She paused as though hesitant to continue, then forged ahead. "You, of all people, should know. Ivey is a powerful and skilled Guardian. She's close to completing her training and will bond to a Finder soon." She paused again, seeing my reaction. "You have thought of that, right?"

As soon as she said it, I felt like I'd been punched in the gut. No. No, I hadn't thought of that. As a matter of fact, I hadn't considered that at all. I had been more concerned with learning how to control my abilities, studying with both the Priests and the Guardians, and thoroughly enjoying what small amount of time Ivey and I had together to consider much beyond a few days at a time. Plus, with all this mess with Shaggy... No. I hadn't considered that I was about to lose her.

"Yes, of course," I muttered, feeling numb as I stumbled past to find Master Gwynn.

I found him in his office and shut the door behind me. He was scribbling on a parchment and held up a finger for me to wait as he finished his task. When he finished, he stoppered the ink, cleaned his pen, and set the parchment aside to dry.

"How did they take it?" he asked.

"Well. They support my decision," I said. "Or at least if they disagreed, they didn't show it."

"They are good men. I've known them both a long time." Master Gwynn smiled sympathetically. "I suppose you will have more time to study the deeper mysteries of the Priesthood."

"About that," I said, an idea beginning to form in my head. "How hard would it be to learn to be a Finder?"

Master Gwynn's eyebrows rose. He was hesitant when he continued, uncertain where I was going with this. "I'm afraid it doesn't work like that, Son. Their abilities, much like the Guardians, are more specialized. Their power more finely tuned to the duties they must perform."

"Both the Keeper and Tamil said that I had the potential to become a Priest and a Guardian. So, why wouldn't I be able to be a Finder?"

"For the same reason you can't learn to be a Bloodmage," he said. "As a Guardian, you can draw on your own spirit and use that to your benefit. As a Priest, you can draw on the spirits of others."

I nodded."Like Helen and little Iela."

"Yes, and for that reason, I believe you will be an amazing Priest." He paused a moment. "Death rites might be a bit of an issue, though."

"Because I eat souls?" I asked.

"Yes, every soul you consume seems to strengthen you, make you more powerful. Perhaps that can be avoided, though. It will require testing."

"I am not interested in testing that just yet, Uncle."

Master Gwynn nodded his understanding.

"So I can't just learn to be a Finder?" I asked.

Master Gwynn shook his head. "Finders are very rare. They see the soul's substance in such fine detail that they can determine whether that person has the potential for magic. They do not draw their power from the Goddess, thus they are the only ones who can directly battle necromancy."

I opened my mouth to protest further, but he interrupted. "There is something else that needs consideration."

"What's that?"

"The blood bond," he said. "It is a link between the souls of the Finder and the Guardian. What would happen to you if someone were directly linked to your soul? What effect would it have on them?" He shook his head. "No, my boy. I don't think that is an experiment I would be willing to undertake at all."

I hung my head. There was no way I would subject Ivey to my Aspect. I left quietly, my hopes dashed.

Later that night, I held Ivey and we cried. Then we made love. Our hearts were broken. It was that night that we said our goodbyes, each understanding that our paths could not continue together.

She, like me, had been focused on the smaller battles, the here and now. We overcame the obstacles directly in front of us during the day and celebrated each other's victories at night. We gave no thought to the future. Neither of us could imagine a life outside the Order or even the temple gates. But we knew there was much in store for us, if not together. Had we only known how much.

Aspected

Ellyn was right. It wasn't long until Ivey had her Finder. I congratulated them both at the end of their bonding ritual. Her Finder, Ered Rowley, seemed a good man and was apparently one of the most powerful Finders to come through the school in some time. I didn't know by what they measured such things, but I hoped for Ivey's sake that it was true. She would have to rely on him to watch her back, just as he would have to depend on her.

She looked so happy, finally having achieved her goal. I was jealous, if I had to be honest. It thrilled her to have succeeded at her dream and she was looking forward to the beginning of her service to the Order. I was still poring through ancient manuscripts and rituals to learn what I needed to play the Priest.

I was proud of her. She had worked hard to get where she was, and she deserved every bit of support she could get. None could say that she had not earned the title of Guardian. She was strong, fast, supremely skilled with any weapon she picked up, and she would serve the Order well. I owed it to her to be happy for her, and I didn't have to work hard to do it.

Being proud of her was especially easy when I saw her for the first time in her new Guardian's armor. She was on horseback in the courtyard. She looked magnificent and dangerous in the brown leather bands and tall boots. Her hand-and-a-half sword rested comfortably on her hip alongside a dagger that she could reach with her off-hand. She looked dangerous and ready.

She caught me staring with my stupid, proud smile and returned it with a smile of her own. It was a smile that emphasized her excitement that she was not only beginning her travels, but that she got to share a small portion of them with me.

She and Ered were to start their journey today. They would travel in search of children that could wield magic, while keeping constant vigil against darker powers.

They would take to their own road after a short task: protecting me. Well, not just me, but my group. I had been selected, along with the rest of the senior Apprentice Priests, to attend the temple in the Capital City of Corinthia to complete the final lessons of the Priesthood under Celate Darius. It would take four months to complete our training, and I had nearly everything I owned in two large bags, as did the rest that were riding in the wagon.

Ivey said something to Ered, then maneuvered her horse up next to the wagon.

"Are you excited?" she asked me.

"Yes. I am very much looking forward to this. How about you?"

She beamed a proud smile and nodded. She leaned forward and spoke across me to Ellyn. "Take care of him, will you, Ells? He's a bit of an idiot."

Ellyn smiled and nodded. "I promise."

Caught between the two of them, I was completely off guard. "Hey, wait. Don't I get a say in all this?"

"No!" both women said at once, then burst out in giggles. Ivey rejoined Rowley, and they led the procession through the main gate of the Grand Temple and toward the causeway.

Master Guardian Brenn was there along with his Finder, Mistress Cilia Lesalt, an enigmatic character who was a legend in her own right among the Finders. She had supposedly defeated no less than five necromancers during their time on the road. This was before they both returned to the Grand Temple to teach. Mistress Lesalt seemed at once cordial and aloof. She peered down her nose at everyone equally like a grumpier female version of Brenn. I thought they were well suited for one another.

Magister Haran brought up the rear, talking animatedly with Master Gwynn. Uncle Tamil had elected to return with us, stating that he was needed in the Capitol and this was as good a time as any to return. He said that he had been with us too long as it was, no matter the respite from his duties he had enjoyed during his stay.

Ellyn sat next to me on the driver's seat while Ricio and Gauwen rode in the back. It became her claimed perch. She had relegated the other boys to the mounds of baggage. Of the original class of Apprentices I had joined with, only Greymond Thewe was missing, having taken the trip last year. He had returned and made no delay in departing for a temple on the other side of the Empire, eager to begin his journey.

I couldn't blame him. I was eager as well. This would be a milestone for me, a completion of a thing I had worked long and hard to obtain. I would be a Priest. It was an exciting and frightening proposition. I had volunteered to drive the wagon. It would give me something to do during the two-week trek north from Drada.

We were five days out of Drada, and Ellyn was bouncing the seat springs in her excitement, just as giddy for the road as the day we left. Her mood, her very personality, was contagious, and she chattered endlessly. It was refreshing, and I found myself smiling more often than not.

"What are you going to do once you get back from the Capitol?" Ellyn asked.

"What do you mean?"

"Well, you'll be a full Priest then. What kind of posting do you want?"

"Oh," I said, finally understanding what she meant. "I've been thinking I would do the traveling Priest bit. I think I would like to see a bit of the Empire. Go to more remote villages that don't have the luxury of a Priest and see what good I can do there. What about you?"

"I definitely plan to request a position at one of the large temples," she said. We'll see how the Capitol is. Maybe I could just stay there. I hear it's beautiful. There is so much to do there. I'll bet it is wonderful. Maybe you could travel that way, for an extended stay, maybe?" She smiled up at me sweetly.

"I would like that very much. It would be nice to see a friendly face in a big city, I think." I smiled back at her.

That made her bounce more.

Snap.

My head shot around to the sound of its own accord. A twig breaking as though underfoot, perhaps?

"What is it, Evan?" Ellyn asked.

I said the first thing that came to mind. It was one of Master Brenn's sayings. "It's either an animal or an ambush." The second part of the saying came unbidden to my mind: 'Until you know better, assume an ambush. It's better to look the fool than die the fool.' I grabbed Ellyn and threw her to the floor in front of the driver's seat and covered her body with my own.

Just then a searing pain streaked up my back. A quarrel from a crossbow. I cried out, and Ellyn screamed, as did nearly everyone else in the procession. I rose and turned to identify my attacker. I caught a bolt in my chest, just below my left collarbone, for my effort. The impact threw me from the wagon. My only thought was that the archer was close. Damned close. I landed with a *whoof* as the wind was knocked from my lungs, and even over the agony in my chest, I heard my name.

"Evan!"

It was Ivey. I rolled my head to the side, dazed, to see her frantically defending against three attackers. Beside her, Ered Rowley, her Finder, struggled to regain his feet with an arrow shaft protruding from his thigh and another in his shoulder.

He raised his hand, a vicious sneer on his face, and one attacker fell dead with no apparent wound. I saw what happened, though. He'd ripped the man's soul cleanly from his body. He paid for it, however, as he fell back to the ground.

Ivey, sword in one hand and dagger in the other, stood over him, blocking strike after strike, eyes swirling with grey smoke.

I struggled to my feet. The bolt shaft had broken off in my tumble, but I could feel the iron head grate against bone. Out of habit, I drew on my power to give me strength and felt the grating lessen, then disappear altogether. I looked down and saw the broken shaft still protruding through my bloodied brown travel robes.

I couldn't believe this was happening. Didn't they know there were Guardians escorting us? Didn't they know that Priests were off limits in battles? That was why I'd become a Priest to begin with, damn it all—to be apart from this. *I gave this up so I don't have to be a killer!*

I drew deep on my spirit and leapt across the wagon to catch the axe that descended toward Ellyn's head. Her eyes were wide in the realization that she was dead. I crushed the hand that wielded it, then brought the axe around and buried it in skull of the man who had brought it to bear. His head split like an overripe gourd, and I felt not a thing. No emotion. Nothing. I should have felt remorse, shouldn't I? I should have pitied the life he could have lived, but I didn't. Then I felt anger. How dare he attack me? How dare he attack my friends? Rage bubbled in my chest as the bonds of my Aspect stretched, and it howled for release, for revenge.

I refused. I bound it ever tighter, as Master Gwynn had taught me. I couldn't let that ravenous beast loose on anyone, even my enemies.

Why? Why shouldn't I kill them? Are they not my enemies? They attacked me and mine.

The answer was plain. I didn't have the right to claim their lives. That was reserved for the Great Queen herself. If Hessa wanted their lives, she could have them. Who was I to get involved?

It seemed everyone screamed at once.

Ered was struggling back to his feet a second time. He took a blow to his wounded shoulder and fell back to the ground before tearing the soul from the man and discarding it like the wrapper of a wintertide pastry.

My mouth watered at the waste, and I felt ill at the realization.

Master Brenn and Mistress Lesalt fought back to back. Each wore a manic grin and danced around each other like they had done this a thousand times. I had known Master Brenn for ten years and I had never seen him so calm. Mistress Lesalt, for all her sixty-odd years of life, looked positively lustful in the mayhem she created on the battlefield with her magics.

Uncle Tamil fought sword and dagger against two men and looked to have them well in hand. I noticed his eyes, too, were hazed in grey cloud. At his feet, unmoving, lay Master Gwynn.

More men closed on the wagon from the trees nearest the road. One grabbed Ricio and started to haul him over the side. Ricio cursed, punched, and kicked, but caught a slap from his attacker. Ricio stabbed the man in the forearm with a belt knife he pulled from somewhere. This earned him a punch, which left him dazed.

They'll kill him. They'll kill my friend. They'll kill them all. They're monsters.

The laughter bubbled from my chest again, and my strange harmonic voice sounded eerie even in my own ears.

"They don't know what a monster is, but they will."

I dropped to shadow and felt my clothes and the iron bolt head pass through me as I sped to save my friends.

I materialized just in front of Ricio's would-be abductor and plunged three silver talons into his throat.

"Mine," I hissed and ripped it out, spittle peppering his slack face as he fell.

Another had Ellyn by the ankle and was dragging her from her spot in front of the driver's bench. She kicked at his face with her slippered foot, but he laughed at her. I appeared behind him and, grasping his head between taloned hands, twisted. His neck snapped like a dry twig.

"Mine."

Two spirits drifted in front of me. Two souls, once desperate for life, now reduced...to food.

I drew them to me and felt a rush of strength. The wound in my shoulder began to close.

I looked to my friends. The struggle of holding my Aspect at bay was intense. It wanted nothing more than to run, hunt, kill, and feed. "Run to the Masters!" I screamed at them as they gawked at my Aspected appearance. I shoved them toward Brenn and Lesalt. Gauwen was dead.

The loss one of mine to these bastards infuriated me, and my Aspect responded. The hunger for the hunt was nearly overwhelming.

Tamil had dispatched his and had gotten Master Gwynn to his feet, half dragging the dazed man in the same direction that I had sent the two Apprentice Priests.

I started looking for work.

Several lay dead at Ivey's feet, but she was wounded, having been overwhelmed from the start. It had forced her to play defense, and her foes wouldn't let her get her feet under her. She wouldn't be able to last like that. She needed a breather. I grabbed at the shadows and pushed them toward the two that Ivey still struggled against.

One lost his focus as my shadow passed over him. He took a vicious cut from Ivey's sword. The other disengaged and looked about himself in a panic. The last thing he saw was my silver teeth coming from the shadows to claim his soul. I threw his broken body aside and looked Ivey and Ered over.

Ivey was bleeding from several minor wounds, but could still fight. Ered was down, but conscious. The pain from his wounds was evident, his eyes glazed and senseless. I moved on with a nod. Master Brenn practically screamed in my memory, 'The best care for the wounded is to kill the damned enemy.'

That was precisely what I resolved to do. A fresh batch of men were coming from the east, as though someone had called in reinforcements. It stood to reason that rest of the attackers would be in that direction. I jerked my head toward my intended direction. She nodded in acknowledgement, her breathing nearly back under control. I dropped into the shadows and spread myself out in an ever thickening fog. Those I did not kill with blades of shadow ran straight into Ivey's merciless sword.

Thirty feet inside the treeline, I saw them. There were many already on the road engaged with my friends, but there were more here. They huddled in nearly organized groups of five and ten. Another group skirted the road looking to flank Tamil and Brenn, who had the Priests between them, and they, along with Mistress Lesalt, were hard pressed. If that group made it around them, none of them would survive the day.

Time to hunt. I thought, then further loosened the bindings on my Aspect and leapt into the middle of the nearest squad.

I tore into them with teeth and talon. The surprise on their faces turned to fear as a monster out of their nightmares ripped their friends to shreds. Their screams got the attention of their fellows, and all heads turned to me.

I dropped the last corpse to the ground and exulted in the influx of spirits that rushed into me. My body and mind buzzed with power.

I let out a roar that came from everywhere and nowhere. My strange voice made it seem the very trees were alive and vengeful. They tried to scatter, to flee the monster in their midst.

Those that could muster the courage to move their feet fled and died. Those that couldn't, died where they stood. I hunted, and killed, and fed. None escaped. Not. One.

I MADE MY WAY BACK TOWARD THE ROAD. I WAS COVERED IN GORE AND quite satisfied with my hunt. I made no sound as I passed between the branches and stepped onto the dirt track, my black tongue cleaning the last bits of meat and blood from my talons. Tamil and Master Brenn had two of the attackers bound at their feet. Mistress Lesalt gasped and flung out her hand.

"The Lost!" she screamed.

"No, Cilia," Tamil cried, but it was too late. Her power struck my chest right at my heart. It was a thin tendril of shadow. I felt her pull. It wasn't my soul she encountered, but my Aspect. I snarled a warning as my taloned hand closed over the shadow embedded in my chest and grasped it tight in my fist. She flinched in surprise and pain, but she held on.

"Soulless beast," she snarled and prepared another lance of spirit.

"I have a soul, Mistress," I said, my harmonic voice seeming to originate from all around us. I asserted my magic and visualized wrapping my Aspect in bands of power. My skin turned from the deepest black to my normal hue, and I lost a few inches in height as I stood naked in front of her, holding on to her power as though it were a curious plaything. "I just fear that it is broken."

I gave the tendril a tug, and the Finder staggered forward, eyes wide in horror. When I released it, it retreated into her where it belonged. She stood there gaping at me.

"That's impossible," she whispered.

I shrugged, then, realizing my nakedness, drew a hand over my head in a circle and shadows flitted about me, taking the appearance of living robes. That seemed to intrigue the Mistress greatly. She stepped up to me, her fear forgotten, and extended a slender finger, lifting my chin slightly until I met her eyes. I didn't flinch away, even as I felt her power trickle into me. My Aspect reared and prepared to strike at the intrusion, but I silenced it with an imposition of will. I trusted Master Brenn, and by extension, I trusted Mistress Lesalt, at least to a point. But I didn't think this was an attack. I knew that Finders could sense the truth in someone they looked into. She left her finger in place, the point of contact cool under my chin.

"Impressive," she whispered. "How did you do this?" She made to caress my writhing robes, but her fingers passed through to my bare chest. Her fingertips smeared the blood that painted my skin.

"The shadows," I held out a hand as they played about my fingers. "They obey me," I said simply.

"These are no shadows, boy. They are souls. Many souls, from what I can see."

"I know."

"And yet, you not only wield them as weapons, you command them. You can touch them. You grabbed my very soul when I attacked you. Why didn't you kill me?"

"This is the boy I was telling you about, Cilia, Master Brenn said. Her face registered recognition, but her eyes never left mine.

"The one who quit the Guardians because he killed someone?" she said in surprise. "I sense what you have done here, boy. All this death, and not one loose shade in sight." I nodded. She had the right of it. "But they aren't loose, are they? You have them. You have them all. I ask again. Why didn't you kill me when I attacked you? You could have without a thought."

I nodded again. I could have killed her, though what I did was pure reflex, instinctual. All I would have had to do was pull and her soul would have slipped from her mortal body and she would have collapsed like those that she and Ered had killed.

"You're not my enemy," I said. "You just don't know me. It would be wrong."

"And those out there." She nodded toward the trees without breaking eye contact. "Did they know you?"

I looked in to the swirling mass of shadow that filled my hand and smiled. "They do now."

She shivered, then spun on her heel and walked away, chin in the air. "I like this one, Tomas. I would keep him were it not for your infernal 'no strays' policy. Regardless, get him back into the Guardians. Your lot needs someone with his strength of character."

Master Brenn grunted.

Uncle Tamil looked thoughtful as he processed the exchange.

Just then, my heart leapt into my throat as I heard Ellyn scream.

The Sacrifice

My eyes still glowed silver when I arrived at the source. I slid to a halt at Ivey's side. Her eyes were closed, and her breathing, ragged. There was a large gash under her arm, just at the top of her new armor, and dark blood pumped from the wound staining the dirt beneath her.

I grasped the armor at the seams and, strengthened by my magic, tore the heavy laces as though they were thread. "Ivey," I cried. I took a strip of cloth from her cloak and pressed it to the wound, but it was not enough. I tore another.

Her every breath came as a labored gasp, then her eyes fluttered open, and her bloody hand grasped at my face. I tucked my chin to capture it, not daring to release my futile attempt to hold her life inside her failing body.

"Evan?" She smiled, looking confused.

"I'm here, Ivey." The words caught in my throat.

Her eyes widened in sudden fear. "Ered!" She looked for her Finder. She had collapsed next to him. He was unconscious but breathing steadily.

"He's alive," I said. "He's hurt, but he is alive."

She smiled. "I did it. I protected my Finder."

"Yes," I sobbed. "Yes you did." Her eyelids fluttered and closed. Her hand fell limp from my chin, and her breathing became even more labored and shallow.

"Somebody help her," I begged. I looked around. Ellyn was hugging Ricio and crying uncontrollably. Ricio stroked Ellyn's hair in an automatic motion. I looked to the rest. Every face told the same tale. Mistress Lesalt and Master Gwynn looked on in sympathy. Tamil and Brenn had brought their prisoners over and were the last to arrive. They took in the scene, and they both knew what was happening.

Ivey was dying.

Ivey was dying, and there wasn't a gods damned thing I could do about it.

"There are four Masters of the Order here. Can't one of you do SOMETHING?" I screamed through the tears that streamed down my face. They all lowered their eyes, not able to bear the accusation in my gaze. They were powerless to help her. I knew that. None were Blood-mages. For all the might of those gathered around, we were powerless.

Uncle Tamil stepped forward, pity filling his eyes. He placed his hand on my shoulder, "Son, it's over. There's no—"

"Don't touch me!" I screamed and slapped his hand away. "Help her, damn you!"

"Evan..." He shook his head sadly, and I saw his heart break for me. There was nothing he could do.

My shoulders slumped. I heaved great mournful sobs as I bowed over Ivey's body, my own convulsing with sorrow. Her fading breath was the lightest tickle. I remembered that feeling—her breath against my skin as I laid awake holding her close to me, her soft snore in my ear.

"There may be a way," a voice sounded behind me.

I raised up to see Master Gwynn push his way between Tamil and Brenn.

"What?" I choked out.

Master Gwynn cleared his throat and said it again. "There may be a way."

"How," I demanded, grasping onto whatever thread of hope could be found.

I gently lowered Ivey's head to the ground and, stuffing the torn tunic into the bloody gash, stood to face the Master Priest. He shuffled his feet under the gaze of everyone gathered around.

"How, Master?" I asked again and grasped his robes, begging beyond hope for the slimmest chance.

He raised his hand and pointed to my chest, hesitantly, as though afraid. He moved his hand closer and tried to brush away the shadows that made up my living robes. I looked at him questioningly, but I willed them to move aside for the Priest.

He placed his finger where the arrow struck my chest. What had been an arrow wound was now merely a red welt.

"I saw you get shot," he said. "Your Aspect healed you as you took in more souls." He looked at Ivey, who was mere moments from Hessa's embrace.

"Bloodmages give of their souls to repair damage to the injured and ill," he continued. I nodded my understanding. "You heal by taking souls into yourself and letting them supplement your own. The soul ever does the healing. With the Bloodmage, he gives. In your case, you take. The result is the same. More spirit might save her."

Mistress Lesalt didn't look convinced. "How do you propose this, Oren?"

"I can't give," Master Gwynn said, staring at me.

"Take from me," I said eagerly. "I will gladly consent if it means saving Ivey."

The Priest shook his head. "I cannot. Your soul, your... souls," he said, glancing at my robes, "are yours. They are bound to you now and forever. I don't have the power or the ability to do it. It would require another unbound soul."

I looked at him for just a heartbeat, then bent and retrieved Ivey's dagger that had fallen from her grasp when she fell. I rose and walked to the nearest prisoner and grasped his hair. I bent his head back and slit his throat before he could even cry out. Blood sprayed in a wide arc across the ground.

Gasps sounded all around from the gathered witnesses.

As the first tendril of spirit exited the man's dying body, I grasped hold of it and jerked it from his still breathing corpse. I held the wriggling, writhing shade in my fist. It squirmed to be free, to return to its Queen whence it came. I denied it in favor of my pleasure.

I stood and held it out for Master Gwynn. "Here," I said, "use this one."

"Necromancy!" Mistress Lesalt cried.

"No," said Gwynn. "She…isn't dead yet."

"A technicality," huffed Lesalt. "At best you will be excommunicated."

"But this valiant young lady will be alive to witness it," Gwynn said. "At worst, I am a misguided fool."

Lesalt huffed.

"I cannot hold it," he said. "You will have to help me."

He knelt down beside Ivey and loosened the lacing on her tunic enough to lay his bare palm between her breasts. He started praying. The prayer was familiar to me. It was the same prayer he had used when trying to retain Helen's spirit. I watched, however, as Ivey's soul began to drift from between his fingers.

"Now," he said, urgency filling his voice. "Force it inside."

I did as he instructed, and he released the ritual spell abruptly, causing her body, and that of her Finder, to buck savagely.

Their eyes flew open, wide enough that it seemed their eyeballs were threatening to pop. Both of them convulsed. Their backs arched as one, and they screamed in such pain that the memory of it would break my heart over and over. As much as it would haunt me in the years to come, however, I could not bring myself to regret it.

I SAT FACING THE FIRE, MY BACK RESTING AGAINST A LOG. I STARED INTO the flames and considered this day's events and my part in them. Ellyn was wrapped in her blanket. Her head laid in my lap, and my fingers trailed gently through her blonde curls as she slept.

Ivey and Ered slept in the wagon, which had been rearranged to accommodate them. Both were resting peacefully. They would live. Ivey was still in bad shape. Their injuries began to heal almost immediately, but neither had healed completely. Master Gwynn believed it was because they shared the soul through their blood bond. Her wounds were mostly closed and were now dressed, as were those of her Finder, who had been in a little better shape to start with. She was stable. It would suffice until we made it back to the temple and the Bloodmages could attend them properly.

Tamil staggered over, bottle in hand, and sat down hard next to me. He offered me a drink. I shook my head. I wanted to feel whatever it was I was feeling at the moment. I deserved it, though I didn't know what it was I was supposed to be feeling. After a moment of frustration, I gave up and took the bottle and drank.

I handed it back to him as the burn set in. Uncle Tamil had once said that whiskey's burn was the soul healing, but that was not what it had looked like on Ivey's face as she screamed her throat raw. I shook those thoughts from my head.

"What happened with Master Gwynn?" I asked in a soft voice, not wanting to wake Ellyn. "I saw you four have a big discussion, then he grabbed his things and left."

Uncle Tamil took a drink from the bottle and sighed. "We tried to get him to come back to the temple. We promised him we would all speak on his behalf. He would have none of it. He knows how Zai is. What you two did wasn't necromancy, but there were enough ethical considerations that I could turn it into a class by itself. It would likely get him exiled at the very least." He sighed. "So he skipped the trial and left on his own. We all intend to speak for him when we get back, regardless."

"What about me?" I asked.

Tamil shook his head. "No. You just delivered a sacrifice. An unwilling sacrifice, perhaps, but he did try to kill us. And you know? Fuck it. I don't care."

"Even Mistress Lesalt?" I asked.

"Even her," he said. "She agreed with his position once she saw it in action. She holds you blameless, by the way. 'Only a tool,' she said. 'A damned powerful tool, but a tool.' She won't be winning any hearts once she voices her opinion. Then again, Cilia never gave two tits about what anyone else thought." He chuckled. "I asked her to marry me once." He took another drink. "You know that?"

I raised my brows at him. "How did that go?"

He smiled. "She laughed in my face. Said I wasn't man enough to handle her." His smile grew wistful and longing. "She might have been right. It might have ended terribly." He sighed and took another drink. "Hessa's tits, what a beautiful disaster that would have been."

The silence grew between us, but it wasn't uncomfortable. Of my two parental figures, Tamil was more laid back. He was much sterner on some things than Uncle Zai was, but in other ways, he was the friend that knew more than me, and I could talk to him about anything. He cleared his throat.

"So." It was a command. I knew what he wanted. It was the same thing he always wanted when a significant event occurred in my life.

What did you learn? I asked myself.

I looked down at Ellyn's peaceful face as I trailed my fingers through her hair. It was almost dry. She had washed the blood from it after we moved to a campsite a few miles from the battle. We didn't have the personnel to dispose of the bodies, and the predators would be out as soon as the sun set. I thought about the question. I had been ever since I sat down here.

"My power might not be as terrible as I thought," I said.

"Hessa does nothing without reason," he said cryptically.

"You still think the goddess brought this on me?" I asked, meeting his gaze.

"Now more than ever," he said with surety. "What else?"

"My role is not as clearly defined as I would like."

"How so?"

"I am perfectly suited for killing. I mean, look at me, or what I can be," I said reaching for his bottle. "I am really good at the one thing I never wanted to do. I mean, I knew that as a Guardian I might have to kill, but it was never real. It was a concept. Now that I have seen it, I think I should be appalled at myself, but I'm not. I can't really imagine wanting to kill, but I know that it is sometimes necessary to protect those you care about."

Ellyn shifted as I spoke but didn't wake. I smiled down at her peaceful face.

"Have you considered that the reason you are good at it is precisely because you understand the cost?"

I looked at him sidelong and took another drink before passing the bottle back.

"Can you imagine your power in the hands of someone like that Larkin kid?" We both shuddered at the thought. "Just consider for a moment what that would have looked like." He sat there for a time, his thoughts drifting. Or perhaps he was just drunk. "No, Son. I can't imagine a better person to have such skill or power than one who truly understands the consequences and accepts them for what they are." He drank and passed the bottle back to me.

"And what is that?"

"A burden. One born of necessity."

"Is it really necessary, though?" I turned to Tamil. "Is it? I could have let Ivey die. Ered would have lived. And so would that prisoner."

"As far as I'm concerned," Tamil said, "his life was forfeit the moment he attacked us."

I grunted. It was a fair point.

"What else?"

I took the bottle and took deep pull as I caught my mentor's eye. "I learned what I am willing to do to protect those I love," I said. "It scared me."

"Why did it scare you?" he asked.

"Because I don't know that it was right. I only know that I was willing to do it." I took the bottle and another deep pull. "It scared me."

Uncle Tamil's face contorted in pain. "I'm sorry, Son. I'm truly sorry you had to learn that lesson so harshly." He reached for me and pulled me toward him. I rested on his shoulder, and he kissed the top of my head like he did when I was a child.

We sat for the rest of the night, not speaking, and watched the fire before us as it danced against the darkness. We were each lost in our own thoughts, but drew comfort from one another. We passed the bottle and then another until the sun rose and the light of a fresh day chased the darkness from the road ahead.

Epilogue

Tamil Haran, Magister of the Realm and First Consult to the Imperial Court of Arul, strode through the grand entrance of the Imperial Palace. Guards to each side snapped to attention at his passing. He paid them no mind. It was proper that they do so, just as it was proper for him to ignore them. They had a job to do, and engaging with them would distract them from doing it. He had a job to do as well.

He made his way up the winding staircase, passed another set of guards, and entered the passageway that would take him to his office. The guard outside his door opened it, then stood at attention as he entered.

"Idara," the Magister called as he entered the room, "is the Emperor in?"

Everyone in the anteroom jumped. Everyone but Idara. Idara Emryn doesn't jump. There were always several clerks in attendance to the Magister of the Realm. Clerks attended to many of the prime functions of the Empire under the direction of his supremely competent assistant.

"Yes, Magister. I believe he is," the young woman said. "Good of you to send word that you returned, Magister. We are always pleased to prepare for your arrival."

"I didn't send word, Idara," Tamil said, deadpan, as he headed for his office.

"Yes," came the reply with only a hint of disapproval.

"You always have everything well in hand, woman," the Magister said. "There is no need to prepare. Anything pressing?"

"There are a number of dispatches that have arrived in your absence. They are on your desk."

"I will take care of it soon. For now, however, I do not wish to be disturbed."

Idara scowled. "It shall be as though you never returned," she said.

"Excellent," Haran said with a smile as he closed the door to his office and drew the bolt.

He made his way to the far wall and pressed on a latch. A floor-to-ceiling panel popped open, revealing a passage beyond. He slipped inside and closed it behind him with no trace of his passing. He travelled a scant distance and placed his hand on another latch, revealing a similar aperture. He entered to find the man he was looking for scratching at a parchment. The pen made frustrated sounds as it performed its task.

The man was in the middle of his fourth decade. He had broad shoulders and a strong face that reminded Tamil that he was just as stern on the battlefield as he was in his throne. He was none other than his Imperial Majesty Escian, Emperor of the Realm of Arul and long-time friend. Haran moved to a chair and plopped down in it to wait for his friend to finish his scribblings. He leaned back, propped his feet on the desk, and poured a glass of wine from the carafe sitting at the Emperor's elbow.

Tamil swirled the red liquid in the cup as he waited ever so patiently. He was feeling smug, if the Emperor had asked him, which he didn't. Instead, the impertinent bastard finished his missive and set it aside to dry, then scowled at the dusty boots propped on his desk.

"You remember that little project you spoke so adamantly about?" Tamil asked.

"You mean the one you encouraged me to abandon at the earliest opportunity because it was so infeasible as to be ridiculous?" The Emperor pushed the offending boots from his desktop.

"Precisely the one I mean." Tamil smiled and sipped the Emperor's wine. He hummed his satisfaction. "Delicious."

"What of it?"

Tamil Haran poured another glass of wine and passed it to his friend. "There is someone I think you should meet."

The End of this tale—the beginning of so many more.

To learn more...

If you liked Aspected and would like to see what happens next, the story continues in:

The Emperor's Conscience: Book 2

Also in Audio wherever fine audiobooks are sold!

BECOME A VIP MEMBER

If you enjoyed ASPECTED and would like to know more, you can sign up to be a VIP Member.

VIP Members will always be the first to hear about everything: novel progress, release dates, pre-orders, cover reveals, and behind the scenes peeks into the life of The Emperor's Conscience.

Join now at
www.michaelkcombs.com

www.ingramcontent.com/pod-product-compliance
Lightning Source LLC
LaVergne TN
LVHW051003080826
845145LV00009B/2432

* 9 7 8 0 5 7 8 7 2 1 9 4 1 *